ANDREW HOOK h... short stories publis... and collections also... magazines ranging... books are a collection of mostly SF stories, *Frequencies of Existence*, and *O For Obscurity, Or, The Story of N*, a fictionalised biography of the Mysterious N Senada written in collaboration with the legendary San Francisco art collective, The Residents.

ANDREW HOOK

CANDESCENT BLOOMS

SALT
MODERN
STORIES

SALT

CROMER

PUBLISHED BY SALT PUBLISHING 2022

2 4 6 8 10 9 7 5 3 1

First published in Great Britain in 2022 by
Salt Publishing Ltd
12 Norwich Road, Cromer, Norfolk NR27 0AX United Kingdom

www.saltpublishing.com

Salt Publishing Limited Reg. No. 5293401

A CIP catalogue record for this book is available from the British Library

ISBN 978 1 78463 256 4 (Paperback edition)
ISBN 978 1 78463 257 1 (Electronic edition)

Typeset in Granjon by Salt Publishing

This book is dedicated to all those actors and actresses who paid the ultimate sacrifice in defending and protecting the arts and the cinema

Contents

1932

Introduction: H is for Hollywoodland

45ft
1932

H ow did I get (up) here?
The evening forms a cool September, nothing yet to bite. My jacket hangs loosely over both shoulders. My knees, bent in this position of departure, remember those stepladder rungs, the indentations in my soles. Nine months previously, the first official snowfall had been recorded in the United States Weather Bureau's fifty-four year existence in Los Angeles. The snowstorm had begun at 5 a.m. and continued for over two hours.

Today it is I who shall fall.

One foot above the Hollywoodland sign, my jacket

expands like wings, pulling away from my body with inexorable motion.

Two feet off the Hollywoodland sign my shoes hug tight, afraid to let go. One becomes braver than the other.

I hold a breath.

My fingers clench the purse containing the note.

I am afraid, I am a coward. I am sorry for everything. If I had done this a long time ago, it would have saved a lot of pain.

Will my life flash before me? Studies suggest the phenomenon could be caused by parts of the brain that store autobiographical memories like the prefrontal, medial temporal, and parietal cortices.

You know, I've completed my research.

I am Peg Entwistle. An actress about to lose sense of time; memories converging from all periods of my life.

I am P.E.

An actress about to lose.

◊

44ft
1920

Just as Bette Davis had told her mother she wished to be exactly like me, so – in 1926 – did I aspire to Olive Thomas.

I had been recruited by the New York Theatre Guild.

Broadway there I came.

There was success in my twenty-eight performances as Martha in *The Man From Toronto*. Not bad for an eighteen-year-old from Port Talbot. And unlike movies, my mouth ran with words, my scenes developed in colour.

You know, at the height of Olive's fame, the Hollywoodland sign wasn't in existence.

Olive would have no memory of it.

Yet – as I return level – I have a memory of her.

Because she died four thousand three hundred and eighty nine days before me. That's how memories are formed.

◊

40ft
1926

Oh, Valentino!

Valentino.

I am sucked in descent. A sudden punch to the soul. Valentino doesn't acknowledge as I hurtle, snagging stockings on a bullfighter's muleta. The concealment of a sword.

I saw him in *Blood and Sand*.

I will be blood in sand.

Perhaps I might have played Vilma Bánky's role in *The Eagle*. How we would have soared. Perhaps I might have saved myself. Could it be I would have saved him?

Valentino died two thousand two hundred and sixteen days before me. That's how heartache is formed.

◊

36ft
1933

In early 1932 Broadway was already a distant memory.

Boredway.

Even with Bogart.

The films were there – those films – just at the ends of my fingertips.

Perhaps I caught them. Perhaps I was there, at the St. Francis Hotel in San Francisco in September 1921, watching as Arbuckle opened the refrigerator.

Would they have called me that?

Would I have haunted Fatty, two hundred and eighty six days after my death?

◊

32ft
1935

I am most often cast as a comedienne, most often the attractive, good-hearted ingénue. For that reason I might have starred alongside Thelma Todd instead of ZaZu Pitts. But I would rather play roles that carry conviction. Maybe it is because they are the easiest and yet the hardest things for me to do.

So I shrug myself into Todd. The wind billowing her dress as I slip inside, slough her off with my role. Isn't this how subterfuge starts? Whilst here, I play opposite the Marx Brothers.

Laughter carries with my shoe at head height. I flail

towards it, as though it were of the utmost importance.

I die one thousand one hundred and eighty six days after my death. Photoflash.

◊

28ft
1937

I could get used to this. Forcing my way into films, novels. Dotting the I's and crossing the T's.

Pretending to die, one thousand seven hundred and twenty five days after my death: segue from one life to the next.

◊

24ft
1942

If you're looking for something circular, I have it right in my hand. When my thumb flicks vertical I expect to see light.

But unlike Stan Laurel it is *I* who turns somersaults; aflame.

One coin in the air, whilst the leather of my purse contains more money than I will never spend.

The force relaxes my fingers.

Which falls faster: a ton of purses, a ton of shoes, a ton of jackets or a ton of a girl?

Bets are taken on the sidelines.

Heads.

Or tails.

I skew the difference, make a disaster movie three thousand four hundred and nine days after my death.

◊

20ft
1955

I hand Dean a lit cigarette, Laurel's trick after all. The culture is different here. I have come a long way.

I continue to come. In backs of automobiles upholstered with denim.

Eight thousand four hundred and fourteen little deaths.

◊

16ft
1959

We form a comedy act: Entwistle, Reeves and Switzer.

Watch how we fight over our billing.

Carl, George and Peg.

Do I star as Lois Lane or Darla Hood?

Where is the order to it?

Catch me.

Catch me!

I want to be saved. Even on a bed of alfalfa, on average nine thousand six hundred and ninety six days too late.

◊

12ft
1962

I struggle claustrophobic. Hidden within a role within a role.

Peg Entwistle: Some Like It Hot

The billboard pops coloured lightbulbs all around the picture houses.

To play any kind of an emotional scene I must work up a certain pitch: the quality of a sound governed by the rate of vibrations producing it; the degree of highness or lowness of a tone, the steepness.

Have I really made ten thousand nine hundred and fifteen movies? Are honestly none of them serious roles? How can I live with myself. Isn't . . .

◊

8ft
1967

. . . my life just a car crash.

Twelve thousand seven hundred and four car crashes.

◊

4ft
1982

Tell me I was fantastic in *To Catch A Thief*: a cat burglar at age forty-seven.

Tell me I was superb in *Rear Window*: a socialite at age forty-six.

Tell me I was perfect in *Mogambo*: on safari at age forty-five.

Tell me I was in *The Wedding in Monaco*. Tell me it wasn't Grace Kelly.

Tell me I wasn't already eighteen thousand two hundred and sixty days dead.

◊

0ft

1932

How did I get (down) here?

Well, it's a long story.

The hiker who finds me wraps up my jacket, shoes and purse in a bundle and lays them on the steps of the Hollywood police station.

She doesn't want the publicity.

My last role was in *Thirteen Women*. Whilst it was one of the earliest female ensemble films it premiered to neither critical nor commercial success. It was released after my death.

I was released after my death.

I *am* Peg Entwistle.

I committed suicide in Los Angeles off an advertisement for real estate development.

And there are thirteen letters in Hollywoodland.

Thirteen symbols of thwarted ambition.

Memories of Olive

*O*H, MY GOD!
    I was born Oliveretta Elaine Duffy in Charleroi,
Pennsylvania on October 20th 1894. Misinformation
disseminated throughout the silent movie era is that everyone spoke in title cards and there was no colour in our lives.
If this were true then watch me rise from my mother's
womb an ashen grey, my tiny crenulated fingers clutching
the three-lettered sign, *Wah!*

Jack insists on interjecting that whilst life isn't so prosaic
the whirligig of movie making adds sub-strata to existence
unprecedented in other methods of employment. With this
I'm prone to agree.

And in this regard, *caveat lector.*

I open my violet-blue eyes to the pale pink of breast. I
suck life in.

New sensations: the odd transition from carpet to floor-
board, the planed-smooth surface of my wooden rattle, the
aroma of foodstuffs I am as yet unable to eat, those birds

so far, far away, the smell of cold steel on my father's rough hands, his clothing, his destiny.

And in my mouth. Everything. In my mouth. Right now.

Oh, my God!

What I remember about 1906:

The Great San Francisco Earthquake smudged in newsprint, buildings crumbling onto my twelve-year-old fingers.

Pride in white-chalking this spelling of the Monongahela River despite twenty-seven variations. My fingers touching my tongue on the return to my desk.

Twice the population than there is now.

The electric theatre. A silent trigger.

0.8 square miles of land. 0.1 square miles of water. That it wouldn't be the Magic City in my lifetime.

The tragic death of James Duffy. My father.

True death is always *tragic, glorious* a misnomer.

Oh, my God!

When I worked at Joseph Horne's department store the L-shaped structure was in two, yet to be three. Six storeys faced Penn Avenue, six storeys faced West. Selling gingham was similar to forays in the movie industry: tiny checks. *Hold your title card now.* I have no recollection of the three-sided clock. I remember the six-story electric Christmas tree occupying a place on the corner of the building at Penn Avenue and Stanwix Street. I remember the crowds, gawping.

Jack insists on interjecting to add that this building was at McKees Rocks. He expects to know my life better. There are three variations of that spelling, too. The oldest human bones in eastern North America were discovered here during an excavation. None of them were mine.

My wage was $2.75 a week. In your time this might buy you a Mission tortilla, a box of Mrs. T's Potato & 4 Cheese Blend Pierogies, a cantaloupe, some tissues. Total: $2.64 plus $.11 tax = $2.75.

I might have gone to the pictures.

When Bernard Krugh Thomas proposed I didn't really know what I was doing. All I took out of that marriage was his surname. I'm sixteen with nine years remaining. Two spent with him.

Oh, my God!

New York is just so.

So.

And the people so.

My aunt took me to the Armory Show on Lexington Avenue between 25th and 26th, sometime between February 17th and March 15th, 1913. I bought a circular button with blue edging and a stylised green tree as its centrepiece. Select here a title card – in red – reading *The New Spirit* to signal the change in my life. I was an astonished American. Fauvism, Cubism, and Futurism: there was none of that in Charleroi or McKees Rocks. Approximately 1/5 of the artists showing at the Armory were women, many of whom have since been neglected. Jacqueline Marval / Kathleen McEnery / Katharine Rhoades. I ate colour.

My aunt introduced me as a model. No longer a salesgirl in that gingham dress. *Fuck*, I won *The Most Beautiful Girl in New York City* contest. Fuck (*title card*)! I was on the cover of the *Saturday Evening Post*.

My own life: a dream of make-believe.

Jack is here again. Pointing out that some reports suggest Fisher introduced me to Florenz Ziegfeld, Jr. – *the glorifier of the American girl* – whereas my recollection is that I walked straight in and asked for the job. Sometimes he's uncomfortable that I made my stage debut in the *Ziegfeld Follies of 1915* on June 21st. Sometimes he's even more uncomfortable that I was cast in the *Midnight Frolic* show. But I'm his. I wasn't then, but I forever will be.

Besides – *yes please* – money in my clothing. No change, please. Title card: *she was chaste and chased*. Pass that white correction fluid for those black pages of history. It could be cold on the roof garden of the New Amsterdam Theatre. But – oh! – the lights. Each one a pearl. Each pearl bought by German Ambassador Albrecht von Bernstorff. All ten thousand dollars ($10,000) worth.

My worth.

And in my mouth. Everything. In my mouth. Right now. *Oh, my God!*

"Head back."

Brown hair cascading – *oh how it cascades* – to shoulder length. Red barrette, just so. Eyes closed. Lips parted. *What was I thinking?* Visible upper set of teeth. Jack: *delete set, sounds false*. Pale pink rose twixt thumb and ring finger. Black silk gown bunched, on the slide. Such exposed flesh. Breathe in. *Breathe in*. Left breast clutched (echoes of *Wah!*), nipple palmed. Right breast exposed: a masturbatory tool. Such sweet scent.

Topless portrait of Olive Thomas (*Memories of Olive*), painted by Alberto Vargas for Florenz Ziegfeld. Current location unknown.

Oh, my God!

So this was how it was: model, stage, screen. So many of us. I was a girl like that.

And here comes the Santa Monica Pier. I shouldn't remember the carousel hippodrome, but I somehow do. The Pacific Ocean roils beneath us. I was young, romantic. *Jack says I still am.* We loved to dance. Nat Goodwin owned a cafe and cabaret, *Cafe Nat Goodwin*, right on the pier. It looked like a battleship. We were there a good few years before the sun set. I was young, wildly happy. *Jack says I always was.* And Jack was such a beautiful dancer. You can quote me here. You can quote me here in full.

Jack is a beautiful dancer. He danced his way into my heart. We knew each other for eight months before our marriage, and most of that time we gave to dancing. We got along so well on the dance floor that we just naturally decided that we would be able to get along together for the rest of our lives.

Like those artists at the Armory we did things different. We announced our engagement a year after we married. *Surely a title card here?* It wasn't always black and white. I refused for my career to be hidden in his shadow nor propelled by his limelight. I am my own person, yes. No question. And all the movies came.

My wage was $2,500 a week. In your time this might buy you two Smith & Wesson model 17 classic pistols, one thousand two hundred roses, twelve leather top hats, eight thousand seven hundred and thirty packets of potato chips, two thousand nine hundred and ten candy bars, or eleven white leather biker jackets.

I was in the movies.

Oh, my God!

Like everyone I knew, I wanted serious roles. Jack: *There was only so much you could do, baby vamp. No need to have gotten into a flap about it.* He jests. I made *The Flapper* in 1920. The first movie to portray the *flapper* lifestyle; my lifestyle. We were seen as brash for wearing excessive makeup, drinking, treating sex in a casual manner, smoking, driving automobiles, and otherwise flouting social and sexual norms. I played a sixteen-year-old farm girl sent to Mrs. Paddle's School for Young Ladies (I am *not* making this up)(someone else did), who gets embroiled with the fast life of an older man. It was comedic. It was my most successful film. I loved it.

Intermission: Misinformation disseminated throughout the silent movie era is that everyone's lives were lived to the accompaniment of piano music. I'm told the best score for *The Flapper* is that by Robert Israel who was born long after my death. Kids need to grow up.

Oh, my God!

I love you.

I'm sick of arguing.

You know Olive.

Know what?

You know Olive you?

What?

Olive you Olive.

Fuck you Jack.

Olive / I love / anagram.

So? Physalis is almost syphilis, you gooseberry, but that's not what I meant when I told you to go out for fruit.

If – *if* – we fought – maybe it was over this.

We fought plenty.

We made up plenty.

We fought plenty.

It cost us plenty.

I enlisted *to impress you.*

And look how that went, Jack. Look how it went.

Title card: *their marriage is on the rocks.*

I confess. I discussed it with *Flapper* writer Frances Marion. Frances, I said, I argue with Jack all the time. Our filming schedules keep us apart, and when we coalesce we find we've held back the arguments just as much as we've held back the love. He's got this *boy next door* image but his life is one of drinking and drug abuse – and womanising – that's gonna culminate in the severe alcoholism that will result in an early death.

And she said: *You're two innocent-looking children. You're the gayest, wildest brats who ever stirred the stardust on Broadway. You're both talented, but you're both more interested in playing the roulette of life than in concentrating on your careers. As a couple, you're strangely drawn.*

And I said: I don't want to remember anything. I want to live a life with no future and no past. I want to time travel permanently in the present.

And she said: *Your movies are your time travel.*

And I said: Most of those movies will be lost because they're shot on combustible nitrate film which is going to suffer massive acid deterioration. Either that or they'll be destroyed in fires caused by the nitrate film itself.

And she said: *You're making this up. Your films are your memories. That Vargas painting is your memory. We never had these conversations.*

And I look – *I look* – and I say, no, we never did. But – *oh boy* – I wish we could have done.

I was alone in the industry. I brought my brothers into film with Selznick. William worked as a cameraman while

James worked as an assistant director. But I couldn't talk to them privately. And the Pickfords – they always held me at a distance. Even the brightest stars can be dead inside. I danced. I loved to dance.

Jack insists on interjecting: *We danced in the Montparnasse Quarter of Paris. Our second honeymoon.*

Forgive me. Forgive me, Jack, if I regret that.

Oh, my God!

Jack jumps from the bed, runs across the bedroom into the hotel bathroom and catches me in his arms. In his absence, the bedroom an empty scene with nothing but the Paris moon straining a 3 a.m. glimpse through partially closed curtains.

In my mouth. Everything. In my mouth.

I gesticulate to the bottle, my outstretched fingers tipping it to pirouette on the marble surface. Close-up on Jack's face: *the horror!*

Title card: *POISON!*

Jack pulls me backwards into the bedroom. He reaches for the telephone and calls for a doctor. Back in the bathroom Jack fills glass after glass with water. He separates egg whites from yolk and forces the mixture down my throat. He jams his fist in my mouth. *Olive. I love. Olive. I love.*

His head jerks. Someone at the door. Halfway to it and a doctor enters with a French ridged-leather Gladstone bag. Their movements become accentuated. Their faces whited-out, their clothes black as silhouettes. Flecks of deterioration pepper the scene. A hair enters the projector as the doctor pumps my stomach three times. Somewhere, in a quiet Montparnasse bistro, a piano is playing. Perhaps a game of cards is in progress. One man is going to work. One woman is going home.

I cough and part of my soul is jettisoned as if recalled on a leash across the Atlantic, lodging itself within the New Amsterdam Theatre, precipitating future rumours of a haunting.

TRIVIA: When I am transferred to the Neuilly Hospital, the Doctors' names are Choate and Wharton, coincidentally the nom de plumes of a once famous now forgotten English vaudeville act.

The doctors tell Jack that I swallowed bichloride of mercury in an alcoholic solution. The solution burned through my throat and stomach. The concoction is lethal, it will paralyse my kidneys. Jack's eye make-up is smudged like the newsprint figures transferred onto my fingers during the reportage of the Great San Francisco Earthquake. Or as devastating as the future atomic shadows of a Hiroshima yet to be dreamt of.

I lie in a liminal state, full of ambiguity and disorientation. There are no cocaine parties, no fights, no suicide attempts, no transference of syphilis. I am not murdered for money or infidelities. I am starring in my final production. It's not black and white and it's not silent. I have memorised the script – me, Olive Thomas, about to die in Paris, France on September 10th 1920, aged twenty-five years old – I have memorised the script for the first talkie I will never make. Here they are, my last lines: *I'll be all right in a little while, don't worry, darling.*

Jack nods – as he interjects – then – eventually – he doesn't.

1926

Honeypot

As HAD BEEN common with terminal patients in my time, doctors did not advise of the certainty of my condition. In a moment of lucidity I chatted about my future. Perhaps they were surprised to hear my voice – I had been silent for so long. Pola wasn't present, but a nurse – doubtless pretty – shaved her head around the doorframe as if to see for one moment longer – for the only possible moment – the rise of my chest.

Still life as a cinematic still.

I gave out.

Once my cells became deprived of oxygen their acidity increased and so began the process of self-digestion. Enzymes leaked from the deterioration of cell membranes, beginning in my liver, then my brain, and eventually all tissues and organs. Damaged blood cells began to spill out of broken vessels and, aided by gravity, settled in my capillaries and small veins, discolouring my skin. My body temperature dropped to that of my surroundings.

Stiffening started in my eyelids, jaw and neck muscles, before working its way into my trunk and then my limbs. The remainder is conjecture.

I wonder if she is attracted by the odour. The smell of death that consists of over four-hundred volatile organic compounds in a complex mixture breaking down the tissues of the body into gases and salts. I hear footsteps on marble. There is a repeating pattern to her black clothing, the red rose, to the veil that masks a multitude of identities.

She whispers: *Rodolfo Alfonso Raffaello Pierre Filibert Guglielmi di Valentina d'Antonguella.*

I remain immobilised. It is astonishing. Ninety years after my death: they still come for me.

◊

Yet I came to them.

On the day I arrived in New York President Woodrow Wilson signed an act creating the Federal Reserve System as the central banking network of the United States.

It didn't take me long to run out of money.

The girls buy dance tickets at ten cents each. Natural selection. I am exotic and playful. There is an energy when I touch them which lifts them off the ground. We are surrounded by displaced members of the European nobility. In later years, taxi-dancing becomes tawdry, but for us – in 1914 – for the duration of a ticket – for the duration of a song – we are coupled. We are a couple. There is purity to transience, unsullied by decay.

Everyone likes me. Everyone is not like me.

Blanca!

Valentino!

Perhaps it is not good to infuriate the husband of a Chilean heiress. No matter how unfaithful he might be.

Valentino!

Blanca.

No one will dance with me after the scandal. My legs fall out of practice. I lose the ability to glide, to turn my hips around a circle. *Valentino* – my friends ask – *what will you do now?* I consider my talents, and when Blanca fatally shoots her husband, I join a travelling musical, leaving the bloody walls of New York for the fine sand of the West Coast.

◊

An Italian sky transposed over Los Angeles. Broad streaks of bright blue immolate my memory. I am here yet not here. At the Musso & Frank Grill at 6667 Hollywood Blvd I eat Fettuccine Alfredo, a recipe brought to the U.S. by film stars Mary Pickford and Douglas Fairbanks. I wonder to myself: what is the difference? I am the genuine article.

"Have you considered the movies?"

Norman Kerry made *Manhattan Madness* with Fairbanks. We become roommates at the Alexandria Hotel. Kerry watches me dance, watches me teach. We coast in a borrowed car, the approaching storm bruising the inviting sky in an agitation of purple. I swing the wheel in a tango of decision. Kerry grips upholstery.

"See this road as your future," he says. "It's all mapped out. All you need is to follow."

I nod once. Assertive.

We cruise a panic of girls.

A rip in the wind tapestry shifts the car sideways in a solid block of air.

The sky emboldens me. We circle the storm. Kerry holds onto his hat. Darkness descends in a sea lion slick sliver of nitrate film, a black beast of understanding, guncotton flammable. Sunlight punches in defined projection through broken squares of cloud. It takes but one drop to fall for the rest to follow. We burst our dam. Laughter takes us. Yet the storm is out before I find confidence to park.

◊

"You think I'm a gangster?"

"You have to create the mould before you can break the mould."

"That wasn't quite my question."

Kerry puts up his feet. Afternoon light falls diagonal. We're going on eighteen months since that storm. He says: "Wallace Reid is the archetypal All-American star: light eyes, fair complexion. You're the opposite. In the movies, they want it black and white. Take Sessue Hayakawa. Don't you *want* to be the exotic, sexually dominant foil to the righteous hero?"

"What about you?"

Kerry wet his moustache. "I'm the matinee idol. That role is mine."

I mix a drink. ¾ oz blended scotch / ¾ oz blood orange juice / ¾ oz sweet vermouth / ¾ oz Cherry Heering. "I'm not looking to be typecast. Those anonymous heavies . . . I don't want a career in interchangeable bit parts."

"You were great in *Eyes of Youth*."

"Anyone would have been."

"Don't sell yourself short."

"Don't sell yourself, period."

Kerry laughs. "You sure you're in the right business?"

And I'm not sure. I'm also not sure when I marry Jean in a union that we never consummate. She will lock me out of the hotel room on our wedding night – engorged with semen – as she releases herself on the bed to memories of the lesbian love triangle she had foolishly tried to put aside.

I could never be part of the sewing circle, only the lavender marriage circuit.

I say to Kerry: "I'm returning to New York."

Kerry says: "See you in two months."

I doubt it, but he shakes his head. He can see the draw, the compulsion, the necessity.

◊

Pestilence.

War.

Famine.

Death.

My future isn't so bleak.

I finish the book by Ibáñez and immediately check the trade papers. Film rights had already been bought by Metro and in a circle of fate I discover June Mathis was seeking me out for the Julio Desnoyers role. A film within a film. This is how I tell it to Kerry who echoes a nod of understanding as though it were scripted all along.

June made me a star.

Overnight I become the *Latin lover.*

A honeypot for the female sex.

This never happens: I rent a room pseudoanonymously. Women queue 'round the block, nose to tail, nipples to buttocks. They bicker in the elevator. Eyes are scratched. Down the corridor they come, one after the other, entering my hotel room to impale their pudendal clefts on my permanently extended member. As they ease off, sated, I provide them with a souvenir: an art deco dildo inscribed with my initials. I kiss each as they leave, my lips' indention creating an impression they will never be able to replicate. I spoil them – permanently – for other men. *Thank you, Valentino*, they breathe. *Thank you for making us feel like virgins again.* I smile, then with one stroke I am ready for the next.

After my death, Mencken published in the *Baltimore Sun*: *Here was a young man who was living daily the dream of millions of other men. Here was one who was catnip to women. Here was one who had wealth and fame. And here was one who was very unhappy.*

This never really happens: I am a closet homosexual. Women cannot see beyond the artifice, I am the epitome of romance; whereas men – reluctantly – sense I am something *other*. They exit disgusted. I become vilified for my pomaded hair, my clothing, my effeminacy. There is an incident surrounding pink talcum powder and the feminisation of the American male. I bend for cock both ends. I challenge a journalist to a boxing match. I enter into another pointless marriage. I carry critical newspaper clippings in my jacket pocket. I compose a book of poetry using the automatic writing technique. I suffer from daydreams even at the height of my success.

"Ignore them Valentino."

Winifred Shaughnessy, known by her stage name, Natacha Rambova, disliked by my friends and business associates, who ostracises me from numerous soirees and influential events, becomes my second wife.

◊

Shake it baby, shake it.

"In this movie, which – if I may say so – solidifies your image as the Latin lover, you play an Arab tribal leader who demands control over the headstrong Lady Diana Mayo, yet ultimately your two disparate characters fall in love. Tell me, do you think Lady Diana would have fallen for such a savage in real life?"

Valentino catches his reply, considers it. He is a European male born of French and Italian parents, with a somewhat swarthy visage enabling him to effectively play exotic roles. He swallows his knee-jerk response, then softly spits: "People are not savages because they have dark skins. The Arabian civilization is one of the oldest in the world . . . the Arabs are dignified and keen-brained."

The interviewer smiles. "Even so . . . do you think the movie is a plausible representation of such a relationship? At the end, doesn't the Sheik's doctor inform Lady Diana that the Sheik is not an actual Arab, but of English and Spanish parentage, brought up by that race after the death of said parents in the desert? Do you think this sits contrary with your rather noble views?"

Valentino folds his arms.

"And in your next role, isn't your character given a foreign name and Spanish background solely to ensure your continued bank-a-bility as the aforementioned Latin lover?"

Valentino leans forward: "In America, are we not all émigrés displacing the original dark skinned inhabitants? America itself is a land of exotica. Even under the crystal-line-bright Los Angeles sky a thread of despair is interwoven by the suicides of those who thought otherwise. You cannot impose the strange on the familiar, you can only reveal it. When you consider that we are all shadows of our former selves then the reverse must also be true."

Following their conversation, the interviewer – *of indiscriminate gender* – takes Valentino's hand and places it there.

◊

I wake craving authenticity. Sweeping the red blanket from Rambova's body she turns upon me, bullish, eyeing my *traje de luces*. I feint whilst she jabs, nimble on my legs. Her knees sink on all fours into sheets the colour of sand. I round, flick the cover to cover her head. Her breasts, her mons: these are her horns. She taunts me: displays. I parry, thrust. We are overseen by a multitude of balconied women. Jealous to the core. Edging. Edging.

I penetrate Rambova and her head shoots back, mouth gapes silent. I stab repeatedly, my hands blemishing her skin. She bucks, forearms collapsing. Further inside, I distend. I am unremitting. She receives me with a little death. The sound excites the crowd. I grip her ankles as she suffocates. Our movements no longer base, but performance art. She submits. My sword, blood slick. I lose count of her wounds and in her final perfect struggle the motion triggers.

From their vantage point the women throw roses.

Rambova's eyes are wet. I run the back of my hand along her cheek. *I'm sorry*, I think, *but* Blood and Sand *should be filmed in Spain, not some Hollywood back lot.*

The injustice is bothersome. Rambova also craves perfection. She becomes an influential art director and costume designer. She backs me in my ill-fated 'one-man strike' against the Famous Players Studio. She aids me in penning my *Open Letter to the American Public*. She interferes on the set of *Blood and Sand*. She creates more trouble than I am worth.

When you fight the studio the studio fights back.

Stan Laurel parodies me as Rhubarb Vaselino.

I admire him.

When we skip a beat on the movies and take up our dance show contract with the Mineralava Beauty Clay Company we surf a new success. Legions of adoring female fans catch a glimpse of me in eighty-eight cities across the United States and Canada. I extend my arms when I bow. Each night amongst the audience one black-clad female licks the stem of a rose. Then there are the séances.

Natacha? Natacha. There is someone here for you Natacha.

Amongst the clientele are those searching for wires, for fakery.

I watch Natacha part her mouth. The resemblance to her press photograph is uncanny. Her trademark black headband carries two cinnamon bun curls close to her temples. Earrings dangle from hidden lobes. Her neck extends. She stares, eyes focussed, anticipating.

Natacha? Natacha. Valentino is here for you Natacha.

I touch my heart but I am not yet dead.

He wants to tell you something, Natacha. Come, Valentino, come. Speak through the mist.

In the enclosed space of the dining room I resolve to be as silent as my movies. The pinkie fingertip of my left hand is connected to Natacha's. She cannot believe this nonsense. The pinkie on my right hand graces that of an industrialist. His wife sits opposite. Her mouth also parted. With lust or wonderment I cannot tell.

He says he will leave you with one dollar, Natacha. One dollar.

Inexorable pressure prevails to prevent Natacha turning her head.

One dollar. In his will. He leaves you one dollar.

I close my eyes. I have more than one dollar in my pocketbook. Is this confirmation of my existence?

Afterwards, in the redeeming cool of night, Natacha remonstrates that I insulted her. I do not understand. At worst, I expected her to be a child-bearing housewife. At best, she was a feminist Egyptologist. Despite the remonstrations of women, it is rare that I understand them.

◊

Monsieur Beaucaire begins a series of box office and critical disappointments that plague me mid-career.

Kerry finds me without Rambova in a quiet moment.

"Laurel has parodied you again, *Monsieur Don't Care.*"

"Yet I cannot hate him for it. He is irredeemably funny."

"That may be so, but it don't make it easy."

"The audiences weren't ready for a period film."

"They weren't ready, period."

"Natacha went into such detail for those costumes . . ."

Kerry sighs. "Maybe so. But if Seventeenth Century Frenchmen dress effeminately then so did you."

"There are more lavish costumes to come."

Kerry leans forwards. *Bar her from the set, Valentino. Bar her from the set.*

When I finally gain artistic freedom to make *The Hooded Falcon* I fall out with June Mathis over her script. Natacha and our cast sail for France to be fitted for costumes. We are there three months and I return with a beard. *Photoplay* publish: *Rudolph Valentino had a beard upon his chin. My heart stopped from beating and I fainted dead away. I never want to come to life until the judgement day.*

I don't know whether to laugh or shave.

The movie is terminated. The name is appropriated for my Falcon Lair estate above Benedict Canyon in Beverley Hills. Four acres in the Spanish Colonial Revival style. Rambova and I divorce. After my death, a mother parks outside my property in a 1929 tarnished green Ford and says: *He had no talent for acting at all.* He had no talent for life. But he was photogenic, and he died *at the right time. Remember, Norma Jean* – die at the right time.

I change birds. Release *The Eagle.* Deny Vilma and I are romantically inclined.

I dance again. Describe a circle.

Shake it baby, shake it.

Sonofabitch.

◊

Then: a soft collapse in human skin. *And*:

it's quite something when a terminal illness takes its name from you. *And*:

when one hundred thousand people line the streets of Manhattan for you. *And*:

when reports of suicides are not greatly exaggerated after you. *And*:

when smashed funeral parlour windows signal an all-day riot for you. *And*:

when an actress claims a posthumous engagement with you. *And:*

It's quite something.

◊

The woman in black is a film historian. She places the rose atop the crypt in such a way that the stem dangles.

Make of that what you will.

First it was Ditra Flame.

Occasionally Pola Negri.

Never Ramon Novarro.

Rose oxide – producing the quintessential Damask scent – is an amalgam of four different chemicals. An unforgettable attraction to a multitude of creatures. Yet a minor alteration can turn the sweet smell sour.

Hear me sing the *Kashmiri Song*.

For they were forever there.

And I.

(Still, they come to me)

I am forever here.

Buckle Up

Fish Tank

THERE'S BUOYANCY TO be found in Roscoe's blood tonight. He floats midway between surface and basement. An anti-gravitational thrum sustains his mass. Propelled through time and space he body-rolls, unencumbered. He might be held in aspic created from his own fat, but the truth is far stranger: Roscoe is experiencing the tremulous cusp of his demise.

The evening boded fortune with Addie jig-sawed on his arm. There was bonhomie in anniversaries and contracts. The summer-edged June heat complimented his internal temperature. He became only marginally damp, and now, in the water of his imagination, he discovers there is an absence of sweat stains. Kicking his legs creates motion; a sensation that's barefoot.

A sensation.

Roscoe is a sensation.

He folds into himself, womb-ready, the movement financing a soft spin. He imagines an overshot baseball locating a city pond, a raft made from empty Cola bottles flipping through the ingress of two ladies, a helium balloon tugging free of its captor. There is surety to his satisfaction, his movements soundtracked by Benny Goodman's treacle-swing, a warm Kinemacolour bleed from black and white. He luxuriates in the absence of weight, aware of more which will follow.

Stretching out – starfish – he extends all directions. Finds barriers.

Puzzled, his fingers spread axolotl-like against glass.

Roscoe bends his knees, kicks, glides.

Somewhere – in this ethereal form – begins the cramp, and the substance in which he is suspended starts to harden.

He jerks within the tank, no longer recognises the difference between freedom and constraint, water and glass. Understands only to take a breath there should be the comfort of air.

Palms flat he circles, his skin slick with algae. On the dry side of the glass: flashbulbs. Microphones. His cheeks bulge with the effort of not talking. There is a liminal state, neither fluid nor sluggish, into which he pleats.

Tightness. So much tightness.

He can't feel his chest.

Is this what it means to . . .

A light bulb moment. Roscoe kicks off the side of the reporters' catcalls and rises, that sensation of weightlessness reasserting, reassuring. He is in the ascendant. Face-forward – fast-forward – into light.

He remembers the best day of his life.

A Hot September Day In 1921 – 1

"Can't you sit still for one moment?"

Sherman winked at Fishback as Roscoe swerved, tarmac zigzagging under the vehicle. They knew he'd sustained second-degree burns to both buttocks from a recent accident on set and lost no opportunity for a ribbing.

"Ah, shaddup!"

Roscoe was in good spirits. He'd been flat out for eighteen months, nine features, three simultaneously. San Francisco beckoned with a triple day vacation. It was all about the numbers. They had three rooms booked at the St Francis – 1219, 1220, 1221 – and spent time counting down the miles from the road signs.

Wedged into the vehicle with the steering wheel shoved against his stomach, Roscoe drove with one hand curving the surface, the other dangling out the open window catching the rays. Occasionally he raised that hand at an oncoming vehicle, almost in wanting – wanton – recognition. The leather seat grew warmer over distance, reacting with his burns as though he wore no pants. Nevertheless, most of the swerves were intended to draw laughter from the rear. Lowell Sherman and Fred Fishback were good pals, between the three of them they were actor, singer, director, cameraman, screenwriter and producer. They weren't immune to a little theatricality. Indeed, it was encouraged.

"You want me to take over driving?" Fishback laughed. "Sherman can sit up front, you can lie out back."

Roscoe framed them in the rear view mirror. "Now why

the hell would you want to do that? I'm paying for this sojourn, least you can do is maintain the role of guest." He shunted hot air from one lane to another, expelling more laughter from his friends. "You both sound drunk when you've yet to touch a drop."

"It's all in the anticipation," Sherman said. "If it bothers you then squeeze down on that gas so we don't have to."

Roscoe decelerated, accelerated. Above, the sky's embrace arced blue. Scrub broke dry soil. Something winged circled. In the desert there was more life than you could see.

"Who've you invited to this shindig, anyway?"

"The usual."

Sherman nodded. Fishback interjected, "The usual hangers-on."

"That an objection?"

"No objection if they're hanging on to me."

Halfway out they pulled into a restaurant, ordered steak with all the trimmings. Cola bubbles scoured their throats.

The Prince of Whales

Hey fatty bum bum.

"Take no notice baby, they don't really mean no harm."

Roscoe couldn't hide behind his mother. Both of his parents were slim, a fact that caused his father to question his seeding. Roscoe's fingers reached out for her palm at the school gates. She shrugged him off. "Can't have me fighting your battles. You've got a lot of fight in you, a lot of grace, you get the balance right and you'll go places none of these kids are ever likely to see."

Roscoe could see little beyond a lifetime of abuse. He

back-flipped in the playground, outran kiss chase, insisted on making a fool of himself before anyone else could do so.

"Go on, through you go."

Hey fatty bum bum.

"Go on baby."

He felt her hand at the base of his spine as she nudged him onstage. The lights were hot. At eight he was the only performer without greasepaint: an impromptu addition. He stood, blinking, toes connected, heels apart. Too young for derision by this older, established audience. Something inside him burst when he sang and when it was over the applause sealed it.

Hey fatty bum bum.

His voice made light work. Nails in his mouth atop a ladder, the anticipation of slapstick a premonition of fame yet to come. He spat the shards into a glove, hammered them into the broken window frame, glass vibrating with each tone.

"You there!"

"Me?"

"Who else?"

Roscoe didn't recognise the customer, paid little attention to who checked in or out less they were female.

"You've got a strong voice on you. There's a talent show coming. Be on it."

Roscoe sat in the wings, watching as a shepherd's crook hauled bad acts from the stage. There was no longer anyone for encouragement, baby. He trod the boards, his handyman's eye picking out fixes. When the crook interjected he panicked, flipped a somersault into the orchestra pit where the jeers changed to cheers from an audience turned feral.

Hey fatty bum bum.

Come with us to San Francisco, sang Sid Grauman.

Come with us to the West Coast, sang the Pantages Theater Group.

Come with us to Portland, sang Leon Errol's vaudeville troupe.

Come with us to China and Japan, sang the Morosco Burbank Stock vaudeville company.

Come with us into celluloid, sang the Selig Polyscope Company.

Hey fatty bum bum.

"I'm not here to get cheap laughs out of my weight. I won't get stuck in a doorway or a chair."

Mack Sennett told me that when he first met Roscoe he skipped up the stairs as lightly as Fred Astaire, and without warning went into a feather light step, clapped his hands and did a backward somersault as graceful as a girl tumbler.

Close friends don't call him *Fatty*. He has a name.

Hey fatty bum bum.

In some countries obesity is seen as a sign of wealth.

The Balloonatic.

The Prince of Whales.

On a million dollars a year there was no need to consume any pies thrown at my face.

A Hot September Day In 1921–2

"I'll bunk with Fishback in 1219, you take 1221."

Sherman nodded. "No doubt I could do with the privacy. What's with 1220?"

"That's the party room."

"Don't you know drinking is illegal?"

"It should be, the way you do it. The alcohol's arriving any minute."

"Can't you make it sooner?"

Roscoe joke-punched Sherman's shoulder then dumped his bag in 1219. He entered the bathroom, wet a flannel, wiped sweat from his face. He wasn't so happy with his bowling ball head and piggy eyes, but there were no replacements. After changing his shirt he entered 1220. Sherman and Fishback were there and so was the alcohol. Bootleg fresh.

"Swig this."

Roscoe sank the contents of the glass Fishback handed him, the liquid burning his throat.

"Boy."

"It's not the best," Sherman laughed, "but it'll do."

Fishback answered a knock, ushering in ladies Delmont, Rappe, Blake and Prevon, alongside gentleman Semnacher.

"Here it is. Here's where it's at."

"It's never more *at* than here."

"Hi Roscoe."

"Hi. Hi everyone."

"How's tricks?"

"How's it going?"

"What are you filming at the moment?"

"My, it's hot in here. Don't you think it's hot in here?"

"I've never known a day like it."

"Doesn't it just burn?"

The air is so thick you could swim in it. Roscoe holds another drink, the contents warming in his hand. These are peripheral people, he thinks, surveying the room. Few of them will amount to much. He wonders how they were chosen – for we are all chosen, in some way, to play a part. He watches himself from the other side of the room, a mirrored duplication. It is as if he is watching a movie, the gilded frame representing film sprockets. There is a slow dissolve as the alcohol is consumed, a gradual debauch to which he is not quite a part. There's a fug in this memory – and it *is* a memory, he realises now – almost twelve years later – as he bobs against the side of the tank which he understands has a semi-cylindrical appearance, the exterior patterned in swirls of red and white.

16 Uses For A Coca-Cola Bottle

To drink from / a makeshift vase / a luminary / a bird feeder / a candle holder / to carry a message / a salt 'n' pepper shaker / wind chime / piggy bank / vaginal insertion / a planter centrepiece / a chandelier / an apothecary jar / a bottle tree / tiki torch holder / hummingbird feeder.

A Hot September Day In 1921 – Triptych

During the afternoon the party began to get rough and Roscoe showed the effects of his excessive drinking. Rappe and I were in our room.

During the party I'd gone to my room to change my clothing. Naturally I locked the door behind me for privacy. I heard a noise from the

Is it possible to be any more sick? Is it possible to hurt so? Delmont shouldn't have brought me here, she knows what I'm like. Semnacher too,

Roscoe came in and pulled Rappe into his room and locked the door. From the scuffle I could hear and from the screams of Rappe, I knew he must have been abusing her . . . Roscoe had her in the room for over an hour, at the end of which time Rappe was badly beaten up. Rappe was a good girl . . . she had led a clean life . . . by the time we forced the door open Roscoe had just about finished up. He had a block of ice/Coca-Cola bottle in his right hand and was using it to forcefully penetrate

bathroom and upon entering I found Rappe doubled over in pain, vomiting. I tried to assist her for several minutes before moving her into my bedroom. She had removed some of her clothing, as she was known to do when under the influence of alcohol. I tidied her up then I sought some assistance from other members of the party. I won't deny I had a history of alcohol abuse but this was under control after I nearly lost my leg. I deny that I'm a gross lecher who used my weight to

he should have my interests at heart. My head is swimming. It's too hot in here. Doesn't everyone find it too hot in here? I don't think I can stand it anymore. Movies: the constant pressure to be; the constant pressure to be someone. I've seen so many toilet bowls from this angle. Why hasn't someone heard my call for help? It's way too hot I need to get out of my clothes. I can't bear these stomach pains. Delmont said Roscoe had mounted me, ruptured my bladder due to excessive weight.

her. He'd torn strips of clothing from her body and she was clearly bruised up bad. I had a life-long friendship with this girl and I'd never seen her distressed. She knew what was to come, she turned her eyes to me and said *I am dying, I am dying, I know I am dying; he hurt me.* Sometimes all it takes to become a monster is money, some-times money just allows a possibil-ity of revealing that truth. It's so hot in here, I think I'm going to faint.

intimidate young girls. You have it on record that I'm good-na-tured and so shy with women that I've been described as *the most chaste man in pictures.* Chap-lin stated he knew me to be *a genial, easy-going type who would not harm a fly.* And whatever Rappe might have been I disagree she was hooked into some sort of *white slavery* racket which enticed girls to Holly-wood promising them anything from movie jobs to money to marriage, then whored them out for profit.

I don't remember this. Wouldn't I remember this? No one knows if I'm pregnant, even me. Roscoe was sweet. He rubbed some ice on my stomach to ease the abdomi-nal pain. I get the feeling I'll be remembered either as some-one's meal ticket or else as some-one's last meal. I'm too young to die. I want the lights, the glam-our; I want the life. I need to be more than the cover photograph of *Let Me Call You Sweetheart.* I want the life, the light. Oh my, how it burns.

A Man Is Nothing Without His Good Name

Fatty!

  Fatty!

  You're going to be arrested for what you did to Virginia Rappe. They're coming for you, Fatty. They're coming for you.

There isn't a cell big enough to hold him. Roscoe's size balloons with each insult, each forceful, bitter attack. There might be no blue and white pinafore dress but there remains the wonder.

  Fatty!

  They'll put you to death, Fatty! Hanging's too good for you.

Roscoe bulks. The camp bed beneath him splinters and breaks. His legs shoot to opposing corners, felled trunks. Palms flat to the concrete floor, his back scrapes plaster from the wall as his head nudges the ceiling. But all of Hollywood is talking. He's the opposite of the elephant in the room.

  Fatty!

  Hey Fatty!

Rape disgusts him. The dropped charge sits uncomfortably in his gut. Guilt would be bearable, but innocence corrupts the soul. Manslaughter is a death sentence but so is accusation. As his size increases, so the clown dissolves.

  Fatty! Fatty!

His feet burst through the floor, his arms smash through walls, his head penetrates the roof. Standing, he manoeuvres through the streets to the court house. Falling debris rains on a sordid-loving city. They got what they paid for.

September 1921 / January 1922 / March 1922 – A Triptych Of Trials

We find that Rappe died from a ruptured bladder & secondary peritonitis. Bruises sustained from rape or heavy jewellery. Roscoe had a smile on his face. There existed fingerprints smeared with blood on a door handle cleaned prior to examination. There is no external cause of rupture. There is no Delmont evidence due to previous bigamy, blackmail and extortion. For as long as Rappe remained lucid and coherent she denied the need

Key witness confirms she was encouraged to lie. New witness suggests historic impropriety between Roscoe and Rappe, discredited as an ex-convict on his own sexual assault charge. New evidence presented on Rappe's promiscuity & heavy drinking: *She was sweet enough, naive. But had no morals whatsoever. She'd sleep with any man who asked her. She was a sad case.* Fingerprint evidence likely faked. The defence so convinced

Acquittal is not enough for Roscoe. We feel a great injustice has been done him. We feel that it was only our plain duty to give him this exoneration for there was not the slightest proof adduced to connect him in any way with the commission of a crime. The happening at the hotel was an unfortunate affair for which Roscoe should be held in no way responsible. We hope that the American people will take the judgement of fourteen men to press charges, contrary to Delmont's assertion. Roscoe's wife shot at entering Court building an outward manifestation of the media assassination. Roscoe remains calm. Deliberation takes 44 hours. Hung jury.

of an acquittal that Roscoe is not called to testify, which jurors interpret as a sure fire sign of his guilt despite evidence of witness unreliability. Media smears sells papers. Deliberation takes 40 hours. Hung jury.

and women who have listened for thirty-one days to the evidence, and are satisfied Roscoe is entirely innocent and free of all blame. Deliberation takes six minutes. Case dismissed.

Buckle Up

Let's make it showbusiness as usual.

He uncorks the bottle. Doesn't cork it again.

The benefit of hindsight is opaque when viewed through glass, the swirled emboss distorts the visual, coruscates light into a miasma of Hollywood dreams and misinterpretations. Memories kaleidoscope and congeal at the edge of his consciousness.

You'll never work in U.S. movies ever again.

He senses Addie on the bed. Her soft murmur a confirmation, a consolation. She is proof that he can love, that he can be loved. She is post-trauma, post-scandal. Yet he dares to speculate a scenario where he and Rappe were romantically inclined. Would she be alive now that he is dying or was it always fated the other way around?

There's a cliché involving actors and bit parts. He's too old but not yet old enough.

How many wives does it take to make a man? How many women?

His heart – pummelled by love, fear, carbohydrates – deigns to ache again. The pain creates a cage that contains him, floating . . . his rubber ring a giant doughnut. He rises to the surface, bubble-powered, the circumference adhering to the neck of the bottle. Trapping him just short of expulsion.

I would like to see Roscoe Arbuckle make a comeback to the screen.

Within soft-space he genuflects.

And here *returns* the buoyancy – here comes the boy – the curl of toes as he arches backwards – vision 360: a motion, a circle – from audience to absence to audience. Into silence. Into companionable applause.

1935

The Ice-Cream Blonde

Jewel Carmen

MY MAID INFORMED me that when she discovered Thelma she appeared unduly lifelike in colouration. Her body was slumped against the steering wheel of her 1932 KBV12 Lincoln Phaeton. She wore a cream silk and tulle dress. One of her high-heeled sandals had slipped and was caught under the accelerator pedal. It was a cold December night, barely two weeks before Christmas. Thelma was wrapped in mink. Her jewellery was cold.

The pathologist took me aside to explain that the colourant effect of carbon monoxide in such post-mortem circumstances is analogous to its use as a red colourant in the commercial meat-packing industry. I think he was hitting on me.

I'm not bitchy. I knew and was not concerned by Thelma's affair with West. They slid and slipped in front of my eyes. I paid no attention to it. When the restaurant began to lose money I might have threatened her. I certainly did if you have any witnesses who say so. I didn't want any part of my investment squandered. Is that so unusual? It isn't only Thelma's death we're investigating. One of my last films was *Nobody*. Looks like there's something to be said for that.

Whatever you might think of me, I *am* a reliable witness.

On 30th April 1913, 8,265 days before Thelma Todd's death, the actress known as Jewel Carmen lodged a complaint that two car salesmen had forced her into delinquency. There was the suggestion of a white slavery ring. Charges were not proceeded with when her age was proven to be twenty-three, and not the fifteen years she had claimed.

Thelma

Too many call me a tramp. I say let those without sin cast the first stone. I will not be found standing in a gravel pit.

And ain't no one ever got a souvenir of my underwear.

Those times were fluid. Sure there were scandals – both Arbuckle and Thomas had fired the salacious desires of the American public – but we were gods and goddesses. We ate ambrosia on Mount Olympus. Spoons in our mouths as we sat looking down from those forty-five foot tall letters. Our cunts wet and our cocks hard.

I sometimes wonder what those hunks in Lawrence, Massachusetts think when they see me on the big screen, my face up real close. Those who had me, and those who wouldn't. Do they brag amongst their friends, or keep silence? How many of their acquaintances were part of my circle? How many relatives? Surely, none of them will say they took the trash out.

Before the man with the dreams arrived I had intended to be a school teacher. I was groomed by the education system to spend my life amongst the innocent. But those beauty pageants and the adoration became sticky addictive and before I knew it I was Miss Massachusetts. That's when you found me. Is that why you've returned? For my life story?

It's getting chilly in here. Can we pause the interview a minute? I have a headache coming along.

Roland West

Alongside my wife, Jewel Carmen, we were co-owners with Thelma of what was to be called *Thelma Todd's Sidewalk Café* at 17575 Pacific Coast Highway. We lived in the large apartment upstairs, in separate rooms connected by sliding doors. It's an open secret that Thelma and I were lovers. We began our affair on a yachting expedition to Catalina Island. Maybe she thought I could take her places.

Thelma was a natural blonde. All the way down. And all the way up again.

The pathologist told me that her lip was bruised.

I asked him if a kiss could do it.

There were rumours that her face was streaked with blood, that her nose was broken, and that a dental filling had been dislodged. In some reports I believe her make-up was unsmudged.

Could a kiss do *that*?

Sure we were volatile / passionate / experimental.

Sure I resented her affairs.

I totally refute the allegation that I might have murdered her aboard the *Joyita* then transferred her body to the garage. We don't run carbon monoxide on the yacht. We don't even run nitrous oxide. That is a joke, right? There are almost three hundred steps from the café up to the garage.

The reason I locked the apartment? I told her she had to be back by 2 a.m. That's when I closed up. That night she was guest of honour at the Café Trocadero at 8610 Sunset Blvd. It was a simple matter of security. Apparently DiCicco had told Ida Lupino that he wanted to be seated next to Thelma at dinner. Why don't you look into that?

You know: she had hands that were so cool that when we interlocked fingers it was like we were already fucking.

Maybe she sought warmth in the car.

Whatever you might think of me, I *am* a reliable witness.

On the 10th November 1955, 7,269 days after Thelma Todd's death, Roland West's yacht, the Joyita, *gained further infamy when her entire complement of twenty-five passengers and crew went missing in the South Pacific. Their fate considered inexplicable on the evidence submitted at the inquiry. Likewise, West's accounts of Todd's death contained contradictions. He said Thelma had woken him, throwing stones at his window. He said she had her own key. Many reports describe him as controlling and possessive.*

Thelma

West directed me in *Corsair* although I chose the pseudonym, Alison Lloyd. I wanted to be taken seriously. When I won Miss Massachusetts I was the beautiful girl with long blonde hair down to her knees. Then I was just down on my knees.

My early silent roles with those comedians were the best. You may have noted I have a sharp sense of humour. Not everyone knows how to handle a wisecracking woman. Maybe, back in Lawrence, I was actually chaste. Maybe I've subjected you to some embellishment. But life is different when you walk through those studio gates: you're doted upon, cosseted, cared for. And once the klieg lights are extinguished you still can't stop the burning inside. I won't deny I've lived my life to the fullest. I wanted to be in the spotlight. They never blinded me or gave me actinic conjunctivitis. I basked.

West knew what made me tick. But also what made me tock. When he refused to leave his wife I did the only sensible thing and ran into the arms of another. You couldn't script it as comedy. Those serious roles turned out not for me. I laid Alison Lloyd to rest. As Thelma I was strapped on the arm of Pat DiCicco. Maybe – for once – I was naïve. I could be an astute businesswoman when required. Other times: not.

Excuse me, but I appear a little dizzy. If my lip is swollen then it's only a memory of marital abuse. Let me touch it with the tip of my tongue. A soft cold bubble of hostility.

Pasquale "Pat" DiCicco

I was the glamour boy of Hollywood. All those bitches loved me. All of them.

A judge once told me you could never legislate in favour of a woman who didn't care about getting knocked around every so often.

If Thelma didn't care for drunken fights, she didn't do much to prevent them. Ain't it the truth that her corpse revealed a .13 blood alcohol reading, and 75-80% carbon monoxide saturation? No wonder her fingernails were intact. Rumours she sank it that night because of me are unfair. Sure, we might have caused a scene, with me parading Margaret Lindsay, my date, at my side, but we were already divorced a year. Thelma wouldn't have killed herself over me. Or anyone.

It broke me up. I didn't marry again til 1941.

So they say I once hit her so hard she had to have an emergency appendectomy. Valentino died from appendicitis round the same time, and I never touched him neither, did I?

In a fight including alcohol your reflexes slow, your reaction time is hindered. You can't even throw a good insult with slurred speech. And no, I never suffered from erectile dysfunction.

Look somewhere else, buddy. So I might be described as a bootlegger and pimp and New York Mob boss Charles "Lucky" Luciano's right-hand man in Hollywood, but

Whatever you might think of me, I *am* a reliable witness.

On the 26 January 1945, 3,329 days after Thelma Todd's death, Gloria Vanderbilt – whose fortune is estimated at four point five million dollars – announces her separation from second husband Pat DiCicco. She alleges DiCicco was an abusive husband who called her Fatsy Roo and beat her. "He would take my head and bang it against the wall," Vanderbilt said, "I had black eyes."

Thelma

The transition from silent to sound-on-film worked in my favour. They couldn't have shut me up too long. Perhaps the technology was developed by an admirer. I signed signatures with a flourish and a wink.

Laurel and Hardy were darlings. We improvised the scene in *Another Fine Mess* when Stan dresses as Agnes. The dialogue might be stilted, but I couldn't have looked more natural. Stan had a boyish innocence, I sported honeymoon blush. There's an undoubted sexual complicity between myself and the audience. My skirt clings to my limbs as though it won't.

I'll tell you something funny. One of Stan's interests was hydroponic gardening. He successfully cross-bred a potato and an onion, but couldn't get anyone to sample it. Stan and I became close friends and he often found work for me when I wasn't working for Roach. He loved my bawdy sense of humour and when I suffered from boyfriend problems, I always confided in Stan.

Roach directed me with the boys, and Langdon, and Chase. I found him overly cruel. He introduced a clause into my contract stating if I gained five pounds then I could be fired. Can you believe such a thing? I've always had weight problems. I've gained and crashed, gained and crashed. Once I passed out on set. Someone gave me prescription diet pills. That was the start of it.

Jean Harlow was given the starring part in *Hell's Angels* because Roach didn't want me to do dramatic roles.

Roach believed the end justified the means. His movies will last. I can't deny it. So will I.

Look, I'll think nothing of this. I can tell that you're a gentleman. But can you place your hand on my heart for a moment? That's right, just underneath this coat. You should detect the beat through my silk dress. Does it seem fast, to you? Or is that yours?

Hal Roach

I gave every opportunity for Thelma to flourish. Whatever I might have suggested was always in her best interests. I would have told her to stay away from DiCicco. I would definitely have told her to stay away from Luciano. But she was a girl that if you told her to be herself she'd try to stay away from herself.

Let's talk numbers. I made seventeen pictures with her and ZaSu Pitts. I wanted them to be the female equivalent of Laurel and Hardy. When Pitts left I made another twenty-one pictures with Patsy Kelly in her role. You see what I'm holding up? That's right. Five fingers. When Thelma died we tried three other actresses but only made five more movies. That was the power of Thelma. She was strong. She could carry people.

Sources will state that when Roland West died he gave me a death bed confession. But that wasn't true. He told Chester Morris, the actor. If that ever happened at all. I persuaded the coroner not to run a second inquest. Either Luciano or myself might not have been so lucky.

Whatever you might think of me, I *am* a reliable witness.
On February 14, 1936, 60 days after the death of Thelma Todd, the Hal Roach directed full-length Laurel and Hardy comedy, The Bohemian Girl, *premiered in cinemas. This*

was Todd's last film – she died after completing all of her scenes – but most of them were re-shot. Roach deleted all of Todd's dialogue and limited her appearance to one musical number: Heart of a Gypsy.

Thelma

I wasn't afraid.

He roiled towards me; walking on his heels to gain height. His slicked back hair combed and set. The dictionary definition of chiselled features. There was some band playing at the Cocoanut Grove. My legs and hips were grooving. My divorce had come through. Pat was gone and West wasn't paying me anything other than business attention. I had a hunger down below that needed feeding.

I edged on excitement. The prescription drugs made me wild-eyed and energetic: the accentuated features of a silent film actress. Everything was heightened. Luciano was untouchable except for those he wanted to touch. I knew only his reputation: Pat had given me that much. He was danger when danger was intoxicating.

His smile was expansive, his arms held wide. He wanted the ice-cream blonde to melt on his tongue.

"Sit with me."

The table was round, angling our knees towards each other. I had shouldered the booze and intended to take no for an answer, but Luciano ordered champagne and when I refused he poured a whole bottle down my neck. Dom Perignon. A good year. He lubricated my throat with his charm. And later.

Reports that my father was bullish and disinterested

might not be true, but the enigmatic older male always did hold some appeal. Too many call me a tramp when I'm just a frightened little girl.

Some days I took him to the Sidewalk Café. He appreciated the wide expanse of the white-painted front, the extensive parking area, the row of arches like showgirls bent over with their asses in the air. He had a particular eye for the unused third floor. Some days, out of hours, he'd put his fingers round my neck and squeeze whilst cool blue light filtered through the windows, putting a glow on everything. His lips were hard and mean. The definition of a gangster. And when he held me like that, I craved to be his moll.

Don't look at me that way.

Look at me this way.

See, I still have the bruises.

Open the door a little. I'm getting nauseous.

Charles 'Lucky' Luciano

You cannot pin anything on me. Miss Todd was a contradictory combination of unliberated punching bag for abusive men and a strong-willed businesswoman. I wasn't the first to hit her and I definitely – put this on record – wasn't the last. I will tell you something, the coroner advised that there were beans and peas in her stomach, although none had been served at Ida Lupino's dinner. This puts your theories to bed. Since when do I look like a man who eats beans and peas?

I will tell you what you know. I approached Miss Todd with a view to utilising her third floor for a business proposition. In the common vernacular, I had already had relations with her ground, first and second floors; but the Sidewalk Café meant so much to her. Like my own business interests, she viewed it as of singular importance. Unlike those movies she made, she had complete directorial input. It was the first thing she had ever owned for herself and she considered it represented freedom. I only wanted to debase her of that.

We had a discussion. Naturally I wanted those rooms for an illegal casino. You can understand my predicament. I liked her in those Marx Brothers movies, *Horse Feathers* and *Monkey Business*. You can tell she had a way with words. I had tried to make her pliant. She had swapped those prescription tablets for amphetamines. I encouraged her career. Yet she persistently refused to help.

One night – and I believe you have this on record, so I'm going to be one hundred per cent honest with you – we were having dinner at the *Brown Derby* when I raised my proposition again. Miss Todd became hysterical. She screamed at me: "Over my dead body!", to which I am supposed to have replied, "That can be arranged."

Hindsight is a wonderful thing, sir. If we each had a cent for someone who made a threat we'd be filling swimming pools with dollars, isn't that right?

Whatever you might think of me, I *am* a reliable witness.

On June 7th 1936, 203 days after the death of Thelma Todd, 'Lucky' Luciano was convicted on sixty-two counts of compulsory prostitution after years of investigation by District Attorney Thomas E. Dewey, and sentenced to thirty years in prison. Ten of those years were served.

Thelma

I might have been loose but I never actually provided sexual favours to advance my career.

I recall that late one night, in those silent times, we had wrapped up the day's filming on *The Traveling Salesman*, and I was invited up to a studio executive's office where a party was in full swing. There were starlets and booze and Paramount men. Clothes had been shed. Maybe I was naïve but I left, not knowing what the decision would cost me.

The next day nothing happened. And then nothing happened again. But it was *never* the case that *nothing* happened.

Roland West – *the* love of my life – should have cast me in one of his noir movies. My life has been a succession of dames, slugs, brutes, and gangsters. The only addition required would be a mystery of unexplained death.

You know something? My headache has shifted like a sulking animal right across my frontal lobes. I probably had too much to drink. Can we get some air in here? Can *I* get some air?

Before I sleep, tell me something. Why are you conducting my interview in this vehicle? You say it's not for *Photoplay*? You say it's research for *Carbon Monoxide Monthly* on the devastating effects of colorless, odorless, tasteless gas? That this isn't some kind of joke?

Then I better get my story straight. You know what Groucho Marx once told me?

Before I speak, I have something important to say.

Groucho

You're a woman who's been getting nothing but dirty breaks. Well we can clean and tighten your brakes, but you'll have to stay in the garage all night.

He see-sawed his cigar.

Whatever you might think of her, she is *a reliable witness.*

On December 16th 1935, the day of Thelma Todd's death.

Thelma

Oh, what are these? Photographic stills? But they're not from *The Bohemian Girl* . . .

Okay.

OK.

And so I understand.

Is exposition necessary?

It wasn't suicide or murder, no. Just some silly old thing.

So; there I am slumped inside that Lincoln Phaeton. My head cradled against the black leather seat. I adored that car. My left hand seems raised towards my mouth as though I wanted to suck my thumb. I probably *did* want to suck my thumb. I've had plenty of car crashes in my life – *hell, some might say my whole life was a car crash* – but I never expected to expire behind the wheel of a stationary vehicle.

And so; there's me on a slab. My skin doesn't look quite natural. Did you know that wax is applied to apples to improve sheen and to seal in moisture? I wonder if I was also hot-air dried. And my hair – I look more brunette than blonde. I can't argue it's me; there's my name, written on the tag. Under those incessantly bright lights.

And so; my post-autopsy picture. No one needs to see this. Naked. Stiffened. An iced-lolly. An iced-dolly. Look at that *Y* of stitches where they put me back together again. I can't reconcile that expression. Can you take it away, please? Will you do me a favour, please? Don't let my mother see this. Have her remember me as Miss Massachusetts, or as Todd and Pitts, or laughing as Stan's feather duster comes apart. I haven't mentioned my mother, have I? Perhaps I should have done. She really was so dear to me.

Are you starting the car?

You know, all I ever wanted in life was to keep my engine running.

1937

Tonight Is Today

*E*VERY MOVIE NEEDS *an opening line. What's yours?*
      Harlean floats through the apartment on a white
chiffon breeze. Somewhere the world is shot day for night.
The distinction bleeds, punches her right in the kidneys.

Other times she might be the actress Jean Harlow,
wearing a white silk chiffon gown, standing on a white
bearskin rug in front of a fireplace mantle decorated with
candelabras and a clock, or perhaps the actress Jean Harlow,
wearing a white silk chiffon gown, curled up on a white
mink fur wrap draped over a damask wing chair, or maybe
the actress Jean Harlow, wearing a white silk chiffon gown,
striding through the forest with a brace of white possum
pelts over one shoulder. Always chiffon, always white.

*Would you be shocked if I put on something more
comfortable?*

She can't always discern the dichotomy.

The apartment is empty. Across the walls her image
flails. Publicity shots each and every one. She runs through

the corridors – from scene to scene without actually making one – searching for the photograph which will indicate to her as she is now. There is discouragement in being one self. Only at Miss Barstow's Finishing School for Girls did she discover her real name. She curled the letters in a notebook, the amalgamation whispering palindromic. She wonders if it has survived, or lies, rotting somewhere.

In the race her gown catches something undefined. Since chiffon is a lightweight fabric that frays easily, she begins to unravel. There is no distinction between material and skin. She twists in the unwind, straightening helio-tropic DNA as it spools in her wake. Organs shuffle and settle like items in a shopping bag. She clumsies.

And if the opposite of white cannot exist without the other, then neither can she.

◊

When pulp artist Jules Cannert illustrated the December 1933 cover of Picture Play *with my image, he provided me with two countenances. Without us having met, he knew me better than anyone.*

Morals are loose terminology. Harlean makes an effort not to judge anyone as she might judge herself. Those who dub her *the filthiest woman ever to have set foot in Hollywood* don't know themselves very well.

She inspects the rushes, leans in the wings. Understands that the head never really has an angle on the workings of the body.

At Camp Cha-Ton-Ka she contracts scarlet fever. Similar to the silver object in a pinball machine it shoots high into her system, before affording a delayed descent courtesy of the ringtones of her internal organs. Occasionally, she lights. More often, the cacophony is silent – although not without resonation. Her mother rows a lake. Maternity ripples. Harlean cannot shake off *The Baby*, no matter how hard the pinball hits. At fourteen she already is a life half-lived. Another step into the white/black divide.

When the MGM publicity team smudges Harlean into grey, photographing her undertaking charity work, in poses of domesticity, in come-clean all-American girl adventures, this transformation from tramp to vamp to champ undermines as Harlean blur(t)s, *Must I always wear a low-cut dress to be important?* Like a hydra, the microphones feed her words to the public body, yet there is no dent to her reputation. She is box-office bankable.

◊

My first movie contract was signed on October 24th 1929, that Black Thursday when the country slid into depression. Doesn't that tell you something?

Harlean leans languorously against the panelling of the Fokker D.VII, one with distinctive mauve and green splotches on the cowling, its engine running. She awaits the only colour footage of her career. She counts her luck against the number of dead pilots, her speaking voice considerably lacking a Norwegian twang. Hughes waves to her from across the lot, igniting a girlish coquette. Already divorced, Harlean considers herself older than her eighteen years, but can mutate younger when needs dictate. The plane's engine exerts vibrations that rumble her body. She goosebumps, without underwear. Always goosebumps. Never underwear.

From a bump to a step.

Lucien Prival walks comically, a smile tumescing his lips.

"Morning Miss Harlow."

She returns the smile, a finger curls her hair.

He rests an arm on the Fokker, careful of the propeller. The backdraft contains them in a coned rush.

"Sleep well?"

"Like an angel . . . in Hell."

Once again, that smile: Prival appears to believe more than she does. She wouldn't – but she wonders what it would be like to – sleep with him.

Eventually she ejaculates: *I like any dog that makes me look good when it stands next to me.*

Prival swivels, takes one goosestep back.

"Use this," he says: *when you lie down with dogs, you get up with fleas.*

One hundred and thirty seven pilots run to their places. Crosses chalked on the earth mark their positions. The crosses of another four rise vertical. Hughes considers these the opportunity cost of filmmaking.

Later, Harlean re-reads her five-year, $100-per-week contract. She is exposed to a singular depression. Undressing is quicker when there are fewer clothes to do so. MGM executive Paul Bern hovers around her peripheries. He shudders her in ways unfathomable. She has already made double whoopee.

◊

I'm not a great actress, and I never thought I was. But I happen to have something the public likes.

Harlean bends double over the sink. In confirmation of her naturally blonde hair she sends clippings to special admirers as keepsakes. The decade is obsessed with knees, skin, and shaved armpits as signifiers of female beauty. Someone anonymous on instructions from Alfred Pagano massages the weekly application of ammonia, Clorox bleach, and Lux soapflakes into her scalp. She squeezes her eyes tight against the stench. She *is* a natural blonde, but MGM don't consider it *natural* enough. Competitions run for beauticians to match her shade. Females chase the impossible.

Afterwards, over toast and tea – and sometimes a cocktail, equal parts light rum and sweet vermouth – she skips reviews. Bern is vocal with the worst of them: *plain awful / plain awful / plain awful / imperfect*. He is less courteous in marriage than he was in courtship. Harlean ticks off his attributes: *plain awful / plain awful / plain awful / imperfect*.

To others she says: *I would have been a magnificent actress if I hadn't always been so lonely. Loneliness saps creativity, especially within a relationship.*

On quiet nights – of which there are few – Harlean drapes herself across furniture, considers *herself*.

I was born Harlean Harlow Carpenter in Kansas City, Missouri. A later change to Carpentier *made me less wooden. I was a Mummy's Girl to the point of abduction. Mummy herself teetered on high heels to the edge of prostitution with studio executives, but her age already had her canned. Perhaps she lived vicariously, but I can't say that she was callous. I was her Baby. I was always all hers.*

I married early into local money, became a socialite. But it wasn't enough to be escorted on the arms of another. When I drove my great friend Rosalie Roy to the studios it wasn't with the intention of usurpation, but there's an awful lot of glitter and light to be had in that neck of the woods.

Hughes wanted me as Blonde Landslide *or* Darling Cyclone, *but it was the publicity director who devised* Platinum Blonde. Honey: I gotta, I gotta, I gotta, I gotta. *Of course, platinum derives from the Spanish* platina, *meaning* little silver. *It has remarkable resistance to corrosion and is considered a noble metal, although its scarcity means that slightly higher abundances can be found at sites of bolide impact associated with resulting post-impact volcanism. Personally, I would have preferred the subtlety of* The Tremor. *But what do I know about showbusiness?*

My public love me, but I dread personal appearances. I'm not one of them. I'm not one of anyone.

Sometimes you can be lonely even when you're wholly yourself.

◊

Some say after the shooting I tarted myself up, kerb-crawled the red-light districts, offered to pay men for sex. To that I say: nothing.

There's plenty of red dust swept up in a storm.

Harlean smokes.

Her husband, Paul Bern, has terminated his existence via the travelling sideshow known as a *bullet*.

Louis B Mayer instructs her to stay low.

Already, she is as low as she can get.

Harlean drinks.

She is tired of being the floozy. When will she get some meat to her parts?

With Gable she is a prostitute. Off-screen she shares him with another. They repeat the partnership, six times.

Hollywood – it appears – is seriously fucked up. Too fucked up even for Pre-C.

Harlean decides to get it down. Rising from the ashes of her husband's death – cleaner than ever – she flames in secret, taps a fiction, molests words into stories, makes something more of herself.

She does this today. She does this tonight.

◊

Don't give me books for Christmas; I already have a book.
chiffon – off – chiffon – off – chiffon – off

◊

Sometimes I'm tempted to go berserk when I read some of the things that are printed about me. But would making a fuss help? I'm sure that would only attract more attention to what was said, and, in the end, make matters far worse.

Harlean considers rebranding. She prints her fore-name and mother's surname on a blank sheet of paper. Rearranges the letters.

Anal Her Harlow / Real Ho Narwhal / Hear All Who Ran / Ah Renal Harlow / All Ran Her, Whoa!

but none snatch her psyche.

Harlean wants to party. She takes up boxing with Max Baer who will latterly be rated #22 on *Ring Magazine*'s list of one hundred greatest punchers of all time, but with Jean all he wants to do is hit the canvas. His wife wants blackeyes. Harlean avoids scandal by marrying a placebo. Yet she wants to party, not live her life with someone rude, sullen and irritable. Within the year she singles again.

She slips behind the wheel of her cabriolet.

Her 6X 2570.

This 1932 Packard was once owned by Jean Harlow, the famous movie actress. Not only did she own it but she drove it. This car is very very impressive. This car, by the way, is all original. I talked to the owner, and he is one of only three people who have owned this car over time. Just think of Jean, driving this. Sitting right here, in this seat. Steering her way, to wherever. Jean Harlow. Wow. I'm attending a social here in Beverley Hills, California. It is a great event. (pauses). Jean Harlow's car. Right here.

Harlean arrives at a party hosted by film producer, Anthony Asquith. She is gloriously underdressed. Chandeliers reflect her candy-top hairdo. Asquith's mother is a stuffy yet acerbic English aristocrat, previously married to a British prime minister. Without realising *Margot* rhymes with *escargot*, Harlean repeatedly pronounces a hard *t*. Lady Asquith – arch – confirms the letter to be silent, just as in Harlean's surname.

Harlow doesn't know whether to laugh or cry or take a leaf from Baer's book.

Names are endemic to her. All that remain are Ruby,

Kitty, Lola, Eadie, Mona, Dolly, Hattie, Helen, Suzy, Gladys, Crystal and Carol.

All those remains.

◊

I came out here a few years ago. I was movie-struck. Finally I got in – but every time they'd give me a test, they would shake their heads and say she's a double for Jean Harlow, can't use her. *And I'd be so disappointed* – Mary Dees, August 1937

There's Gable, Harlow, Morgan, Merkel, Pidgeon and Barrymore. That's *Saratoga*.

Harlean repeats the reel.

She's at the racetrack, her face obscured by binoculars, wearing what looks to be a blue and white sailor hat.

Huh?

She's in long shot. Throws an empty cup to the floor.

It isn't (pla)tin(um).

She's at the table with Hattie McDaniel, wearing headgear as thin as cellulose acetate. The garment is as diaphanous as her underwear isn't.

These cups are just what I need to put my knick-knacks in.

She watches the race in a darkened room, slow-mo photo finish.

Can't they run any faster? I'm dying.

Harlean repeats the reel.

There's Gable, Harlow, Morgan, Merkel, Pidgeon, Barrymore and Dees. That's *Saratoga*.

Harlean notes four minutes of absence.

She repeats the real.

◊

Only an urophiliac wants to taste piss on their lips. I can't say I went that far.

Harlean Harlow collapses in love.

The Powell family lived only a few blocks from the Carpenters in Kansas City, although neither met until their children were established actors. William Powell often wonders – during the forty-seven years he outlives Jean – what might have been. Or if an extension of their relationship would have emerged just as unlikely as that in *Mr Peabody and the Mermaid*.

Harlean kisses Powell as if he were James Stewart.

Repeatedly.

She suffers severe sunburn and influenza.

They make love to *When a Lady Meets a Gentleman Down South*, *It's De-Lovely*, and *They Can't Take That Away From Me*.

She develops septicaemia and has to be hospitalized after multiple wisdom tooth extraction.

They first make plans for an engagement, and latterly marriage. Her belly swells in anticipation of children.

Her symptoms include fatigue, nausea, water weight and abdominal pain.

Yet Powell makes her feel good: brings colour to her cheeks.

She collapses on set.

She feels it in her kidneys.

She cannot count Powell's fingers. Only knows they are not entwined.

Does this happen, or does Powell whisper: *Napoleon*

was killed by wallpaper. Harlean wonders: *ammonia, bleach, soapflakes.*

Then:

Every movie needs a closing line.

Tell me mine.

1942

The Good Girl

I AM THE delicate balance.

We cruise a silver container seven thousand feet over the Nevada desert. There's a clear light. Three abreast: Otto Winkler, Clark's press agent, sits furthest left, alongside my mother, whose shiny sixty-six year-old hand is clutched in mine. Could it be that tremble is caused by outside air pressure buffeting her turmoil? Otto wipes his forehead with a plaid handkerchief. Neither enjoys flying, but I adore it. And we're in a rush. Gable is waiting. There's always a rush when Gable is waiting. Even if I consider it differently – later – with the benefit of hindsight: right now all I have is the beating of a loved heart.

I place a hand on the window, January leans back. The bare landscape basks in crepuscular light. A handful of white settlements glint shell-like as though this sand were all beach. There is something to be said for the perspective of flying. The immediacy.

One moment: somewhere.

The next: elsewhere.

Mother squeezes my hand. I imagine her fingers young, welcoming my world. I have done nothing to disappoint. Perhaps I have succeeded against the odds. If I have a column in the gossips then it's cleanly irrigated. Some would say that's the path of most resistance in the seedy glitter-town of Hollywood. I say it's never difficult to be yourself.

There's not even any dirt under my fingernails.

Our plane creates a shadow across speckled land. Animals run for cover. I wonder whether I would make this altitude had I chosen a bad life. If my guard had been let *right* down? Many choices edge us incrementally. How many of them impact?

Should I have turned left at Albuquerque?

When I see Clark I want to dance. I miss my youth in the Cocoanut Grove, those Charleston competitions. I was more of a flapper than a shlepper. Doing the rumba in *Rumba* was also much fun. Clark would take the lead, guiding my hands with his. Such long fingers. That little moustache of his.

I paid for this flight with a single coin.

This twin-engined Douglas DC-3-382 propliner, registration NC1946, operated by Transcontinental and Western Air as a scheduled domestic passenger flight from New York City, to Burbank, California, via Indianapolis, Indiana, St. Louis, Missouri, Albuquerque, New Mexico, and Las Vegas, Nevada. This twin-engined Douglas DC-3-382.

The mountain rushes us. A splurge of metal, fire, rock.

I wanted to dance.

One moment: someone.

The next:
We do the Potosi.

◊

Or earlier

I stamp my feet to keep the warmth. Mother looks to
her watch. It's 4 a.m. Water vapour in our breath condenses
into tiny droplets which form in the air as cloud. My arms
are wrapped around myself, hands in gloves. Otto moves
from one foot to the other, a lizard on sand. My Indiana
presence has raised over $2 million in defence bonds in a
single evening. The train will take too long. They need
convincing. I make movements with my hands and exude
engine noises through my mouth. Despite their laughter, I
understand they both have much to overcome. Overhead,
lights from similar aircraft compete with the heavens. I
don't want to blind them with statistics, but the train will
carry many more people whose combined odds of accident
surely surmount our chances in the air.

I unclip my handbag, root inside, unclip my purse.

Here, I say, finding a coin. *Heads or tails?*

Otto objects, but my mother creates silences. When she
makes her choice it is with the conviction that she has one.

Or otherwise

I pace back and forth, scour a line in the tarmac. I can't
hang about in indecision. We've wasted enough time in
Indiana as it is. We wouldn't even *be* at war if it was down to
me. Whilst my agent considers these bond rallies to be good
publicity, all I feel is the ache between my thighs at Gable's

absence. His long fingers. That brief moustache. Burbank needs acceleration and watching my mother dither with Otto as an accomplice, as they point to train tickets already purchased as though we couldn't shave some of that $2 million for ourselves makes me aggressive.

I dig into my purse and hold aloft a coin to buy out procrastination. It spins in the air, the interpretation of a chance outcome as the expression of divine will.

Otto catches it in the palm of his right hand, flips it onto the back of his left.

Then there is the reveal.

Mother claps her hands.

I stamp my feet.

◊

Or earlier

When I hear Miriam has dropped from the Lubitsch vehicle I ease myself over and volunteer an audition. Lubitsch takes to my style. He has his finger on the pulse of Hollywood, understands the delicate balance between comedy and tragedy. If he were spinning a coin, he would defeat the angular momentum which typically prevents most coins from landing on their edges unsupported when flipped.

The role of Maria Tura is a smaller part than I am used to, but Lubitsch offers me top billing and whilst I can't say this sways me I do appreciate his gesture.

The Nazis exist to be defeated, and if shining a search-light on ridicule achieves that purpose then I consider it my civic duty to pour myself into the role.

Notwithstanding any of this, shooting *To Be Or Not To Be* catches my happiest moments on film. Let the critics come. I will be smiling as I await them.

Or otherwise

It's no wonder Miriam couldn't work with Jack Benny, she's in her dinosaur years and no amount of archaeology is going to bring *her* back from the dead.

I spend all my time in my dressing room waiting for the Lubitsch touch. But if putting my home up for sale wasn't a clear enough signal that Gable and I are having difficulties, Lubitsch doesn't take my bait. Perhaps his only intention to capture me will be through film.

The movie sucks bad taste. I can't see it going anywhere, but top billing over Benny increases my percentage. And now I've worked at every major studio in Hollywood. Not bad for a good little bad girl from Fort Wayne, Indiana.

I cross one stockinged leg over another.

Five minutes Mrs Lombard Gable!

I flick through the script. Uncap a black marker pen with my teeth, and score through *What can happen on a plane?* There's something to the line which isn't going anywhere, and if Lubitsch or the producers think otherwise they can kiss my lily-white toosh.

◊

Or earlier

Clark?

Hmmm?

Do you think a comedic actress can ever win an

Academy award?

Does it matter? Why don't you try?

Sometimes all a girl needs is for someone to take her seriously.

I *take you seriously.*

When you take me anywhere at all.

We laugh, roll companionably within the sheets. Gable wears cream flannel pyjamas and mine match in flannelette. The only difference being that the weft is generally coarser than the warp.

It's just that *Vigil in the Night* was intended to be my big shot, but I get it that my name doesn't sell tickets to serious pictures. Do you think I made the right choice?

Darling, you're one of Hollywood's highest-paid actresses. You're lucky to have that choice.

I tousle his hair. It's so good to be with him right now.

It's so good to be us.

Or otherwise

I sit at my dressing table, watch Gable pick his toenails on the edge of the bed. He's aging fast, particularly out of the limelight. You wouldn't know there were only seven years between us. Sometimes I wonder if his success holds me back, when I believed it would augment me. I've made comedic films, I've made serious films, I've made a lot of money; but over the past coupla years in the back of my mind I'm seeing myself relegated to the role of Clark Gable's wife.

And whilst I play the part well, it won't win me an Oscar.

Pick those up for Chrissakes!

He's like a wounded deer.

Maybe I *will* make that comedy with Hitchcock. Those serious roles won't advance me, won't make a difference to my life. Yes, the movie with Hitchcock: *Mr and Mrs Smith*, about a couple who learns their marriage is invalid.

Invalid.

Invalid.

If Gable thinks that's sexy then it won't be long before he's the latter of those pronunciations.

◊

Or earlier

I saw how actresses worked. So I copied them. What I didn't understand was that made me a copy of a copy. My slapstick background didn't teach me subtlety. I had timing. Even bad timing.

I wasn't often drunk, but when I *was* the alcohol uninhibited me, loosened my tongue. Hawks pounced. It was the twentieth century, after all. John Barrymore was great fun to work with, but I could tell he hadn't warmed to me. Sometimes I'd hide in my trailer on the lot, wondering what to do with myself.

Hawks was my second cousin. Sometimes only family can tell you what you need to hear. When he arrived at the door of my trailer he had a gold paper star in his hand. I curled in my dressing gown, as though I were cold from leaving a hot bath, but in reality all recoil as he leant against the open door and mimed pasting the star against it.

You're acting like a schoolgirl. And you're too stiff. You're trying to imagine the character and then act according to those imaginings instead of being yourself.

I'm not sure how to be myself.

I said to Barrymore, I said you've just seen a girl that's probably going to be a big star, and if we can just keep her from acting, we'll have a hell of a picture.

What are you really trying to say?

That you need to drink more grenadine, lime, orange juice and vodka.

And then I'll be good in pictures?

Sure, especially screwballs.

I unfold from the sofa. Hunt through my belongings for some cellotape. Pad over to the doorway.

Make the decision to fix my star in the firmament.

Or otherwise

It connected with me that screwball comedies distinguished themselves from their film noir sensibilities through being characterised by a female who dominated relationships by challenging the masculinity of the male lead.

Hawks thought he had me pinned with that schoolgirl remark, but I'm not prepared to be infantilised.

I am as I am.

Ruthless.

All the proof is being drunk under the table.

It's said that alcohol blurs vision, but you need to see through that.

I'm in a bar with Barrymore. He's warmed to me as though I were in his pocket. We chink glasses, elbows rest vertical. If we didn't hold drinks we might arm-wrestle. I expand on my knowledge of the universe.

Right now, all we can see is all that we have. Captured in this instance. And everything here has come together for this moment. This table, once a tree, cut down and cut up and shaped and processed by who knows how many hands. The glass, the drink. These pictures on the walls. The invention of electricity to illuminate and create shadows. The coupling of your parents, the coincidental coupling of mine. The design that's gone into this simple frame of us sitting here, surrounded by all these objects – just as we are now – is staggering. And don't think it's set in stone. It can all be upset in a moment.

I rise – unsteadily – from the table. *Fichte stated, you could not remove a single grain of sand from its place without thereby changing something throughout all parts of the immeasurable whole.*

Barrymore nods, slurs: *This proves to me the existence of a dog.*

I barrel past him, straighten the photo on the wall that's been bothering me all evening. A modern representation of *The Angelus.*

There. Maybe that'll avert a plane crash somewhere.

I see Hawks watching from the bar. He mouths: *honey, that's not even funny.*

◊

Or earlier

I make a picture with good-looking Gable: *No Man Of Her Own.* But in spite of all kinds of hot love scenes I don't get a tremble out of him at all.

Or otherwise

I make a picture with good-looking Gable: *No Man Of*

Her Own. There's a scene where my inexperienced character appeals to the gambler in the more experienced Gable,
getting him to flip a coin to decide whether or not to get
married. The coin comes up heads, and they do get married.

They *do* get married.

Ain't that something to decide on the toss of a coin?

◊

Or earlier

Mother takes me to see William Powell in *The Canary
Murder Case*, in *Charming Sinners*, in *Street of Chance*, in
Shadow of the Law, but it's in *Pointed Heels* with its colour
sequences where I fall for him wholesale.

I think of all those girls gazing at the screen who will
never gain the same chances as me, whose choices develop
no further on what to buy a wife-beater for dinner, or on
which clothes to wear to go out whoring, or on how many
children to pop out of their bellies. Who don't consider
they have any choices at all.

But I . . .

I make *movies* with Powell.

I – *ssssh* – fuck him!

I – publicly – *marry* him.

I pitch my 22yr old carefree, foul-mouthed Carole
Lombard against his older debonair William Powell intellectual sophistication. Such friction!

From the breakfast table I push cornflakes into his
mouth, watch milk traverse his laughter lines, whilst he
folds the newspaper for better ease of reading and intones:
Carole Lombard extols love between two people who are

diametrically different, claiming that their relationship allowed for a perfect see-saw.

Our laughter is enough to wake the dawn.

Or otherwise

When I see Powell up on screen I think: meal ticket. A good-looking fuckable hunk of a meal ticket.

What would you say if I slept with director Richard Wallace to get a role alongside Powell in *Man of the World*?

What would you say if I slept with director Lothar Mendes to get a role alongside Powell in *Ladies' Man*?

What would you say if I slept with actor William Powell to advance my career? Would you call me a good girl then?

There's no doubt my marriage to Powell increased my fame. Our differences created column inches.

Two years of that was enough. When we divorced he blamed it on our careers, but those had little to do with the separation. We were just two completely incompatible people. And you can't find innocence in that.

◊

Or earlier

Carol? Carol?

Mmmm?

Wake up sweetheart. Eggs are ready.

I shift into morning. Mother loves to visit, but her clock is different to mine. I sneak a peak through the curtains. Light piercing my eye as succinctly as the razor in *Un Chien Andalou*. Or so I've been horrified.

I stretch inadequately, the hour making even this simple

movement ineffectual, before snaking downstairs where the smell of food finally disgorges me into the day.

Carol – she insists on calling me this – *have you seen the newspapers?*

I nod, vigorously. *Yes, mother. I was upstairs sleeping off my paper round.*

She chuckles. Warmth radiates inside me. Those eggs start to look damn good.

They've misspelt your name, she says, flopping the review section open. *Carole Lombard in* Fast and Loose. *Carole, that is, with an e.*

Egg melts at the back of my throat. I like it.

Still, mother says, *a rose by any other name . . .*

Or otherwise

Can no one get anything right?

I look hard at the e.

Will changing my name change anything?

Yet I changed it before. From my birth name, Jane Alice Peters, to Carol Peters, after a girl I played tennis with in middle school. That was fine for Vitagraph. Finally I had an excuse not to be a *Plain Jane*. Thanks mother. Then the Fox Film Corporation weren't happy with Peters, so I chose Lombard from that of a family friend.

But Carol*e*? An unintended typographical error by Paramount in the credits of my new movie? That suggested a different kind of choice, one forced upon me by fate.

It dangled something for me to grab.

Would the *e* affect my career, my loves, my life?

Would the *e* offer a paradigm shift towards alternate realities?

I look hard at the e.

Methylenedioxymethamphetamine was first synthesised in 1912.

I take it.

◊

Or earlier

We're just a bunch of seventeen-year-olds out for milk-shakes after dark.

C'mon Jane!

I'm no longer wearing the tubular dresses that were all the fashion only twelve months earlier, those that fell straight from the shoulders over a low, forcibly flattened bust. Now the hem length is rising, the vertical seams shaped to my body, curving out slightly over the bust – accentuating my breasts – and curving *in* slightly at the loosely fitted waist. Such dresses no longer require tight undergarments to follow their lines, now the body dictates the form, rather than the opposite.

This was my revolution.

I've had bit parts in movies where all I've needed is to simper prettily at the hero and scream at the villain.

The car interior is plush. I'm in the front passenger seat. We're cruising, chatting. The night is warm. No coat for me, despite mother's disapproval.

We stop at a red light. The car ahead rolls backward. Slo-mo. When it reaches us – little more than a nudge – our windscreen shatters. Touching my cheek, my fingers come away red from the glow of the traffic light. They're still red in the hospital. My right cheek is permanently scarred,

yet
I'm glad it's the worst accident I'll ever be in.

Or otherwise
We careen around the corner, laughing wildly, our bodies shot full of drink and drugs. His car is on the sidewalk, parked nonchalantly, one wheel on the kerb in a form of solicitation.

Pulling him close I make a play for his crotch as his kisses graze my lips with all the restraint of a bison at a waterhole.

I call him my bison, then.

My big bison.

He leads me to the car. Maybe it's a 1925 Bay State Convertible. Maybe a 1925 Pierce Arrow Experimental Sedan. Maybe a 1925 Brockway E 3000 Pickup. What the fuck do I know about cars? But he has the door open and I'm inside and I'm way off my head, and when I distract him with my fingers and lips he drives into a fire hydrant which shoots its load way into the sky.

Or something.

That's how I tell it before undergoing the plastic surgery which ameliorates my scars and saves my career.

You know something,
if
my life *were* that car crash, then it *was* pathetic.

◊

I release my mother's hand.

She closes her eyes. Smiles.

We're less than fifteen minutes into the last leg of the flight. Gable is waiting in Burbank. My saviour.

I thank the gods for everything that's brought me this happiness. All the tiny decisions accumulated as influence.

Outside the plane, early sunlight illuminates dust trails across the face of the desert, transitory routes created and erased through the natural process of the elements. Briefly I touch my scar, invisible to the naked eye, but traceable under my make-up. Such a small price to pay for everything. This is what I consider, sometimes, that the accident – instead of being a negative – somehow furthered my career.

Yet I don't think the same way of being told to lose weight when I was a *Mack Sennett Bathing Beauty*. Nor do I consider the ramifications of Russ Columbo, who accidentally shot himself cleaning his gun. I don't factor in my pleurisy, or my sterility, or those nervous breakdowns. And not for a second do I recall that psychic who read my palm and told me to *Keep out of planes in 1942*, because *There is danger in them for you*.

I glance down at my thumbnail on my right hand, realise I must have chipped the varnish when I tossed that coin. I rub my forefinger over it, trace the burr.

Maybe that was it. That simple movement.

Or otherwise.

One moment we are somewhere.

The next we are nowhere.

We cruise a silver container seven thousand feet into the desert.

The Easy Flirtations

In Slumber: Thirteen Points Of Contact

Intake to outtake / eyelash to eyebrow / left knee to upper right thigh / right palm to left shoulder blade / right wrist to coil of black hair / left toes to left ankle / nose to left cheek / fingers of right hand to lower back, base of spine / right calf to right shin / taut belly to convex ribcage / right shoulder to upper left forearm / fingers of right hand to curvature of cleft / flaccid to semi / automatic

Maple Syrup

Memories through the amber-glaze of maple syrup. Warm blueberries cooling in the cradle of a silver spoon. Rodeo-sized pancakes frosted with sugar. The widening scent of freshly baked bread. Pork ribs like corsetry through greasy fingers. Hamburgers blood-bled fresh. A cylindrical can of cola-pop. A mess of beans.

Childhood in three hundred and ten days of sunshine.

"Come here baby."

"You're mussing my hair."

A smile to be forgotten.

"We've got to get you ready for McKinley."

"Better than Brentwood?"

"Better than Brentwood."

School flung open windows of possibility. James throws a leather football. Eyes on his mother. Kicking leaves on the return, satchel digging into shoulder blade. *I'll take that.* Her hand in his; both small, one smaller, one enclosed. *I was inside her once / I won't never need to be inside another again.*

Sparks from tap heels. Wood pine fresh. Cosy familiarity. Windows vibrating from scored violin strings. Chin rest snug fit. F-holes yet to snigger. No imagination of a trap such as that wooden body, a cacophony coffin. *One day I dreamt you'd be a performer.* Yet altering size, shape and length of those holes changes the sound, changes the life.

"Watch how fast I can go."

Watch how fast I lose weight.

Sunlight glamorising uterine cancer in a study littered with designs for dental instrumentation. James enters. Sees his father's head in his hands, basketball ready. There are angular shapes, sharp objects. The architecture destined for dissection of a focussed life. A curtain billows. The father raises himself, sideshow real. Muted conversation. Muffled love.

James runs back and forth across the stoop.

Can't you stop that noise?

Apple pie shot with cinnamon. Flaky pastry. Across the way, someone peels a dog from asphalt. In the air, impossibility. A thrumming, humming. The sum of denial echoing a thousand miles.

"Come here baby."

"Don't go, Mama."

The choice is not mine.

James searches for himself reflected in her eyes but the light is not yet right. She is desiccated. This one woman capable of understanding him. Grief exploding like a jealous lover in a dancehall, like a Porsche 550 Spyder flipping a triple across tarmac and field, like injustice administered by a trusted priest. Maple syrup requires both white and brown sugar to boil over a medium-high heat, but for a thicker syrup use two cups of brown.

The Easy Flirtations

They were reported as three eligible bachelors who had yet to find time to commit to a single woman. James might have imagined them as a rock 'n' roll combo, with himself on bongos, Tab Hunter on guitar, and Rock Hudson on vocals. They would call themselves *The Easy Flirtations* and Barbara Glenn, Beverley Wills, and Liz Sheridan would be their back-up singers. In this visualisation, James would play with the men whilst the women looked on. The music wouldn't be beautiful, but it would be harmonious.

The audience would be non-judgmental. James would sit on a high-chair, the drums gripped by the inside of his knees, the taut skin hit by the knuckly part of his palms before letting his fingers bounce off the head. Between songs he would stand, put both an unlit cigarette and a flaming match into his mouth before then removing a burning cigarette. He'd draw on it, sucking the potentiality of so many ghosts into his lungs, before expelling into the audience, misting the crowd. Then Tab would start on the guitar and Rock would glance around and the three of them would merge once again in an intensity of sound belying the spin of the media that rotated the dulcet tones of his former and future lovers.

Amongst the audience, his father would be accepting of the sought approval, and – elsewhere – the vibrations would resonate with the spectral formation of his mother.

Other times, James imagined *The Easy Flirtations* were the headlines the newspapers accepted in a different sort of smokescreen from that emanating from cigarette and match. He was so skilful that his mouth didn't burn.

Mine's A Guinness

James tucked into sausage and peppers at the Villa Capri Italian restaurant on McCadden Street. The legendary restaurateur Pasquale "Patsy" D'Amore had opened the place in 1950 and as James ate he watched Patsy tender to his guests with good humour.

James was feeling grand. He'd just purchased – but had yet to drive – his Porsche 550 Spyder. The silver dream was parked in the restaurant's courtyard, wrapped in cellophane with a bunch of roses tied to its bonnet. It had already drawn appreciative comments from his party. Sometimes he allowed a belief that if he drove fast enough he might catch his mother. The little beauty would make one hundred and fifty with a foot flat on the accelerator, so James had been informed. Even so, it was some velocity from the speed of light.

The joint was packed. Movie stars were commonplace. Monroe and DiMaggio had dated there, both proving heavy tippers. Durante frequented it so often that he had a private banquet room named for him, and Sinatra would head over from the Capitol Records building a few blocks away with his entourage for extravagant parties. Tonight, James understood with some satisfaction, that even with only two and three-quarter movies tucked into his belt he was the main attraction. Not that Patsy allowed ostentation. James was treated to quiet nods and smiles.

Yet despite the ease, his companions' conversation fluctuated his consciousness. Somewhere in the building, gossamer threads were being constructed. At the back of the restaurant, meals yet to be ordered were under preparation. There was an overwhelming sensation of hanging in the balance.

Then: *Isn't that Alec Guinness?*

His eyes roved to the unmistakable forty-something-year-old standing in the foyer, accompanied by an unidentifiable female. The restaurant was full and the staff apologetic. James wiped his mouth, dropped his napkin. In a moment he was out the door, feet slapping the sidewalk, making introductions.

"I was in that restaurant where you couldn't get a table. My name's James Dean. Would you come and join me?"

"Yes, that's very kind of you."

The three companionably retraced their steps.

"Before we go in I must show you something." James flushed with excitement. "I've just got a new car."

He led the older actor to the courtyard, invited opinion. "How fast can you drive this?"

"I could do a hundred and fifty in it."

"Have you driven it?"

"No, I've never been in it before."

James regarded Guinness' expression, wondered if he were seeking approval or validation. There was a strange twilight in the air, when Guinness spoke again James felt he were channelling a role.

"Look, I won't join your table unless you want me to, but I must say something, please do not get into that car." Guinness looked at his watch. "It's now just after ten o'clock on the 23rd September. If you *do* get into that car then by this time next week you'll be dead."

James shrugged then laughed. The man wasn't old enough to be his father.

Love At The Pier

Take my hand.

James ran alongside his mother. Seagull shadows papered the boardwalk. Laughter tore through them, almost visceral desire. His heartbeat beat. A rush of belonging.

They slowed on entering the pier, his mother marginally ahead. Striding from a greater height, she began to pull. There was tension in their limbs, a magnetic umbilical. He took three quick steps, caught her pace. They headed towards the central Hippodrome where the new attraction awaited. The Looff carousel had been replaced by a Parker carousel, James had been shown a photograph of it in the local paper. Thirty-one unique hand-carved wooden features, including two bunnies, four ponies, one sleigh ride and one lovers nest tea cup, rotated at not inconsiderable speed.

His mother dropped to a crouch. *Dare we?* Her eyes captured the light.

He nodded the foregone conclusion.

They squealed as they were sucked around the machine, centrifugal force capturing wild expressions.

Later – after her death – nine-year-old James watched workmen as they installed the neon sign at the entrance to Santa Monica pier, the art deco structure signalling one of those forthcoming changes his mother would never see.

Later – fifteen years later – watching along the length of a dangled cigarette from an adjoining Warner Brothers' lot, James saw the Italian actress Anna Maria Pierangeli.

"It's a sham." William Bast folded the newspaper, quietly. The gossip columns silenced.

"Shut it, Bast."

"It's a publicity stunt. Remember how we were at UCLA?"

"Those days are long gone."

Bast watched his friend pace the hallway. He remembered an earlier interview, when James was less cautious: *No, I am not a homosexual. But I'm also not going to go through life with one hand tied behind my back.*

"There's love between us."

"So it says in the paper."

"Look, what does it matter to you? Pier will be good for me."

"What have you been doing with her?"

James' eyes narrowed, as though searching for memories.

"We rent a cottage on the coast, outside of the tourist traps. Sometimes we sit on the beach for hours, watching the ocean. We talk about ourselves, about movies and acting, about life, about life after death. Sometimes we just want to walk into the sea holding hands so we can be certain we'll always be together."

Bast shook his head. "I can't doubt the best way to walk into the sea is along a pier."

James grinned. "Got to hand it to you Bast, for a screenwriter you sure have a way with words."

Cal Trask / Jim Stark / Jett Rink

In 1952 I gained a place at the legendary Actors Studio, studying method acting under Lee Strasberg. I couldn't help but admire Marlon Brando's languid improvisation and though I reached out the hand of friendship I felt it was little more than smacked away. Carroll Baker was a doll, intelligent and beautiful; is that what you want to know? We were friends but there was nothing between us.

I brought stuff with me to the role of Cal. That fetal-like posturing when riding the top of the boxcar? That was unscripted. Wasn't hard considering the lost relationship with my own mother. When Cal's father rejects the money you know I was supposed to run away from him? You dig that? But I did the opposite. That emotion is real. There's always been an uneasy relationship with my father. You know when I was nine I was sent to live with relatives? I guess you could say that was evident when I was Jim Stark – you use what you bring with you. I couldn't say I was an emotionally confused middle-class suburban teenager – because I wasn't – but then

I was. *You know what I'm saying? Angst rides the sidecar. You know, I might have gone on to be typecast. You notice even* Stark *is an anagram of* Trask? *Some coincidence, huh? An actor must interpret life and, in order to do so, must be willing to accept all the experiences life has to offer. In fact, he must seek out more of life than life puts at his feet. That's why I wanted out of those roles when I took on Jett Rink. Being typecast is one thing, expecting to live it is another. You know I dyed my hair grey in that movie, even shaved some of it back to look like it was receding? I was no longer with Pier Angeli at that point. I'm saying no more on that matter, other than Kazan might have been right when he – and I'm paraphrasing here, improvising, lying most probably – suggested it was an* uncertain relation. *I won't be drawn on other matters, ambiguity makes for a better actor, don't you think? Even after my death.*

Little Bastard

"Hey, you Big Bastard!"

Bill Hickman grinned at his approaching friend. "Hey, you Little Bastard. How's it going?"

"Slow. Real slow. You know I can't race from June through to September? Tied up in this contract. Warners' fears for my life."

"We should all fear for our lives. Without fear there's no frisson."

"S'funny, was talking to a friend 'bout this the other day. Death can't be considered, because if you're afraid to die there's no room in your life to make discoveries."

They slapped each other on the back, half-hugs. "What you working on?"

Hickman ran a hand through his hair. "Gotta couple of stunts lined up. You got time I could show you how to put a car into a four-wheel drift. Does that break with your contract?"

"There's just you and me here, far as I can see."

"So that's what you're saying?"

"Sure. Let's give it a shot."

It didn't have to be illicit but it had to be different. You could go through life like a push-button robot, conforming to society just the way an adequate actor performs for an adequate director. But to get the best out of everything you need to be more than push-button, you need to push.

"Hey you Big Bastard!"

"Hey you Little Bastard!"

"Come over here, get a look at this." James waited whilst Bill sauntered over. He'd parked the Porsche 550 Spyder out of sight on the other side of the lot. James admired Bill, considered him a good friend. He would have been proud of his work on *Bullitt*, on *The French Connection*, on *The Seven-Ups* if he had lived. He'd have been glad Hickman hadn't been put off driving after witnessing the crash, after holding him in his arms as his final breaths eased with some difficulty in and out of his lungs.

"That's some vehicle."

"Take a look at this."

James walked him over to the back of the car where *little bastard* was painted in script across the rear cowling. Hickman laughed. "You Little Bastard!"

James gripped his fist.

Auto Biography

I, James Byron Dean, was born February 8, 1931, Marion, Indiana. My parents, Winton Dean and Mildred Dean, formerly Mildred Wilson, and myself existed in the state of Indiana until I was six years of age. Dad's work with the government caused a change, so Dad as a dental mechanic was transferred to California. There we lived, until the fourth year. Mom became ill and passed out of my life at the age of nine. I never knew the reason for Mom's death, in fact it still preys on my mind. I had always lived such a talented life. I studied violin, played in concerts, tap-danced on theatre stages but most of all I like art, to mould and create things with my hands. I came back to Indiana to live with my uncle. I lost the dancing and violin, but not the art. I think my life will be devoted to art and dramatics. And there are so many different fields of art it would be hard to foul-up, and if I did, there are so many different things to do — farm, sports, science, geology, coaching, teaching music. I got it and I know if I better myself that there will be no match. A fellow must have confidence. When living in California my young eyes experienced many things. My hobby, or what I do in my spare time, is motorcycle. I know a lot about them mechanically and I love to ride. I have been in a few races and have done well. I own a small cycle myself. When I'm not doing that, I'm usually engaged in athletics, the heartbeat of every American boy. As one strives to make a goal in a game, there should be a goal in this crazy world for all of us. I hope I know where mine is, anyway, I'm after it. I don't mind telling you, Mr. Dubois, this is the hardest subject to write about considering the information one knows of himself, that I ever attempted.

"My Case Study" to Roland Dubois,
Fairmount High School Principal, 1948

35°44′5″N 120°17′4″W

The coffee was bitter and the donuts were sweet / *I wish I could say Rolf and Hickman were arguing about whether I should take the Porsche on the trailer, but we'd already agreed I needed wheel time. I'd only had the vehicle a week* / They stopped for gasoline at the Mobil station on Ventura Boulevard / *I don't recall – but I doubt – that we bought any snacks* / They headed north on the Golden State Freeway US 99 and then over the Grapevine towards Bakersfield where they were stopped for speeding at Mettler Station / *If we were going faster maybe I'd be here right now* / They turned left onto Route 166/33, the short cut – *racer's road* – for all drivers heading to Salinas, after which they stopped at Blackwell's corner for refreshments / *Reventlow and Kessler were there. They were good guys. If only we'd been able to have that dinner at Paso Robles* / Taking Route 466 – *I accelerated away from Hickman, I can't remember the reason* – they crested Polonio Pass and headed down the long Antelope Grade. Thirty minutes later a black and white 1950 Ford Tudor made a left turn from Route 466 onto Route 41 heading towards Fresno, crossing the centre line directly in front of them / *That guy's gotta stop . . . He'll see us* / The cars collided head on / *So I tried the side-stepping manoeuvre, racing was in my blood, but I was doing 55 not 85* / Dean's foot was crushed between the clutch and the brake pedal and his body was shunted into the passenger seat fuelling allegations he hadn't been driving / (. . .) / Rolf was thrown from the vehicle / (. . .) / Dean's neck was broken and he received numerous internal and external injuries / *Ribs like corsetry through greasy fingers* / It wasn't long before Hickman and others were at the scene, attempting to extricate Dean from the vehicle / *Cooling in the cradle of a silver spoon* / A woman with nursing experience tried to help / *Blood-bled fresh* / The vehicle was peeled and flattened in the crash / *A scrunched up cola can* / Dean was pronounced dead on arrival at Paso Robles hospital / *A mess . . .* / Hickman confirmed Dean died in his arms / *I'm sorry I'm sorry big bastard.*

The choice was not mine.

In Death: The Point Of Contact

His mother watched as he took an unlit cigarette and a match and combined them in his mouth.

James flared alongside her.

Exactly nine thousand and one days of sunshine.

1959, January

Alfalfa

I LOCATE ME walking behind a police enforcement officer, real slow. His campaign hat at odds with my baseball cap, the raised flap offering to accentuate my forehead. The colours are sepia-hued. My rifle butt rests on my white jacket hip pocket. I hold it mid-length, the barrel pointing skywards as vertical as my former cowlick. There's a canteen strapped to my chest and I notice in replay my fingers unconsciously click it closed. I'm all nonchalant, not there. At fifteen seconds the officer glances backwards. I fail to engage, my jaw set to ignore. When I'm ready for my close-up I realise my features resemble one of those little cymbal-banging monkey toys.

One of *those* little monkeys.

The image is fritzed. I loop it back thirty-one seconds. View again. There is no discernible interlude.

I lean against an on set tree, unidentifiable variety. Curtis is chained to Poitier. We're all the same age, near as dammit. Curtis, Poitier, Billie Thomas, me. There's no real difference between us. I know I could have gotten Curtis' role if I hadn't been a child star. Me and Thomas, our lives both somehow tainted by that early success. When you're a child star no one expects you to grow up. When they meet you they look beyond you, trying to figure out where the *you* that *they* know is at.

I picture Thomas and me in those roles, this film, exploding our myth.

The canteen should capture the bullet, but instead it catapults my career.

◊

C'mon boys, this way.

Thirty-three years after our impromptu audition, my brother, Harold Switzer, by then operating a Speed Queen Company franchise installing and servicing washers and dryers, killed one of his customers in a pointless dispute, then took off to a remote area near Glendale, California and committed suicide. He was forty-two.

I feel a subtle shift in my surroundings at the Hollywood Forever Cemetery as his body is interred alongside mine.

C'mon boys, you do want *this, don't you?*

We burst into the canteen, implode unawares.

Roach is there. He watches us sing and dance. After a while, his slow heavy hands begin a clap. I'm bursting with determination, my six-year-old heart can just about take it. This is the stuff of legends. This is how life is made.

Either way, our parents have got our backs.

Harold has the mark of the strap on his. My injuries tend toward emotional.

Roach calls us over, tousles Harold's hair.

You're easy, he says, *we'll nickname you* Slim *or* Deadpan.

He looks towards me, scrawny and saucer-eyed. His brow furrows. I hold my breath. It hinges.

I jut my chin. Wet my fingers and moisten my cowlick.

You, Roach says . . .

I dance on the spot, my legs kicking backways, sidewards.

You . . .

My father's eyes bore into me like shotgun shells.

C'mon boys.

Eventually, Roach grasps an almost-straw. *You*, he says, *you are* Alfalfa.

I don't understand. Alfalfa sprouts can induce systemic lupus erythematosus in monkeys.

Then someone is whooping and suddenly we're in the air, paraded around the canteen as though this were already a movie. I clutch my hat in a tiny fist. The combination of cafeteria smells is an olfactory melange. We're giddy and sick and a wolf's breath away from the door. As though strobing flicker-book snatches of happiness from the perspective of a fairground ride I glimpse my parents' smiles.

Harold beams at me also, ecstatic.

I nod in return.

This is the start of the movie business: beginner's luck.

◊

The dogs are restless tonight. I have sighthounds, scent-hounds and lurchers. All canines that hunt with – or for – humans.

The air is hot and thick. In one of the adjacent buildings

Alfalfa

Roy Rogers is sleeping. His palomino can sort its own blanket.

I step outside and the dogs quieten. It'll be sun-up within the hour. There's a hunting expedition planned. From within an alcove on the wooden porch I pull out a half-concealed bottle of whiskey and take a sip then a long draught.

There's something to be said for a burning sensation.

Rogers has put several words in for me. I've spent sufficient time in the Eureka Café to feel at home there. Although I wonder if in fictional Mineral City – where 19th-century characters with 20th-century technology aren't explained or justified – my previous sixty-one shows with the *Our Gang* gang would be syndicated without any of those television millions filtering down to the regular cast. Or whether – as is more likely – this exploitation of our earlier prostitution would be just as rampant as in the real world.

I sink more whiskey, wait for *it* to sink *me*.

There are bears out in the woods. Somedays they shit in them.

◊

I do it.

It pains me to sing off-key when by the age of seven I'm an experienced singer/musician. The other kids slip naturally into their roles, but me – me, I always feel that I'm cutting to a different shape. Maybe it's this dichotomy, maybe an inner bullish nature inherited from my father, but I can't help but fuck things up.

He liked to play jokes on people, and frankly none of us thought it was very funny.

My fingers curl around the nails in my pocket. I want to burst Spanky for being an intelligent, gifted toddler. Maybe if he was so deflated then his father wouldn't fight constantly with mine over our screen time and star billing.

I step on other's feet.

I place an opened penknife in my pocket and get Darla to reach for sweets. She cries.

When one of the cameramen tells me to get a move on I persuade our gang to donate chewing gum til we have enough to seize the cogs in his equipment.

They think they don't like me. But I think they do.

George Sidney, senior director, looks me in the eye and says: *When you turn twenty-one I'm gonna get in a cab and find you and beat the shit out of you.*

He won't need to find me. My name will be up in lights, pooling.

Gradually I subsume Howard, like the unborn twin becomes absorbed in the womb. If he doesn't mind becoming relegated to the role of background player, it's only because the burden of family breadwinner is now firmly upon myself.

My mother laid her nest egg.

A sequence of events is more complicated than a string of anecdotes, yet – just as when I urinated on the arc lights – it's only when everything hots up that the stench becomes noticeable.

◊

Dry twigs crack underfoot. I'm walking with James Stewart.

We were together in a wonderful life.

One of the hounds runs a few paces, stops.

I imagine my parents ahead. Stewart raises his rifle, holds a breath.

The hound has long drooping ears which according to some sources means scents are retained longer around the animal's face and nose.

My father exudes tobacco and woodsmoke. My mother wears perfume much cheaper than she believes it to be.

The moment coalesces.

Then Stewart puts down his rifle and we continue.

In the sepia-background, one truck pulls a second behind it. They face opposable, as though the tow-truck has won a tug of war. I can't recall whether I knew of this shot. Trapped within celluloid the moment gains undeserved significance.

Stewart says: *how do you breed with these dogs?*

I say: *very carefully.*

Stewart's laugh comes droll. In that trademark voice™ of his.

I like these wide open spaces, he says. From the vantage point of living in the city.

When we return to the farm I decide to persuade Dian to make love, but for the moment I breathe in the Wichita air and say, *You'll sleep well tonight.*

Stewart regales me with life in the movies, uncomprehendingly emphasising my brief successes, but I don't hate him for it.

I was living here only a few months before I had to connect a radio to the tractor. With money running out like a disturbed lover, and Dian's belly full of future son, my mother-in-law's offer of a Pretty Prairie farm couldn't be refused. Spanky visited me once and laughed, companionably: *you ain't no farmer.*

It's true that I never ploughed many furrows.

You don't enter the industry for pussy when you're only six years old.

◊

C'mon boys.

We're playing adult roles as kids. With all the innocence that contains.

Our gang understands movies cost money. We go all out to get them right.

So what if I can't help but be the outsider, the show-off? Nowadays there'd be a diagnosis for that.

In *Kiddie Kure* we play baseball, breaking the window of a wealthy hypochondriac. His wife seizes this opportunity to get her husband's mind off imaginary illnesses by adopting some children.

In *Hide and Shriek* I open my own detective agency, and re-christen myself *X-10, Sooper Sleuth*. But I fail to discover who stole Darla's box of candy.

In *Divot Diggers* we disrupt a golf game with our gibberish-spouting pet chimpanzee. Chimpanzee.

It's in *Glove Taps* where I meet my nemesis, Butch, for the first time. We clobber each other in a schoolyard boxing match. Off-screen I value the friendship.

One day, Tommy "Butch" Bond and I go for milkshakes. Despite only having worked together for a coupla years he looks to be in his seventies. I order banana shake and – after a moment – he does the same. The interior of the milk-bar is red and white striped. Waitresses flitter in pink uniforms, obscene macrolepidoptera. Neither of us sustain interest. I look to his hands, large and veined. I want to reach out and touch him, knowing my own would be dwarfed in his.

You remember making Bubbling Troubles, he says. *I steal Darla's heart, and you cry in your alphabet soup.*

I vaguely recall *Bubbling Troubles* being mooted as a suggestion for next year's schedule.

You've grown up too fast, I say, blowing air into my shake, populating its thick surface with tiny GeoDomes.

Let me tell you something, he says, *the Hollywood I grew up in used to be a wonderful and magical place, with great folks. Now it is somewhere I would never want to be.*

I want him to expand, to remind me how it will turn out, but instead I look to the window. One of the waitresses is reflected in the glass and cars ghost through her. If I squint I can see her smile.

You were always a smart-aleck, Butch continues. *That's why no one liked you.*

I shake my head. *They love me.*

Then he shakes *his* head. *Not those that matter.*

But I don't care. I'm lost in the age that I'm in.

◊

Even full of whiskey I'm good for high cholesterol, asthma, osteoarthritis, rheumatoid arthritis, diabetes, upset stomach, and a bleeding disorder called thrombocytopenic purpura.

Earlier today I was getting into my car in front of *The Wolf's Den* in Studio City, when a bullet smashed through the window and struck me in my upper right arm.

It doesn't stop me lifting the bottle.

For those who think Dian left me, think again. I have a chequered history of emotional abuse.

If I stand on a ladder will you realise that I'm taller and have been for some time.

I walk unsteady to the refrigerator. A piece of cold chicken squeaks on a plate surrounded by fatty leakage that curves like a question mark. I take it to the table.

Am I to be remembered as a textbook example of a former child star whose life takes a turn for the worse?

Am I to be remembered?

My ego won't accept anonymity.

The first bite of the chicken is inevitably cold, but as I continue eating I find it warms up.

◊

Darla approaches in a long walk. *This isn't real*, she says, and I can't doubt the truth of that.

You were mean to me, often.

I was a kid, I say. *You think I'd do such things now?*

We were all kids. But we weren't all nasty.

I wonder where these conversations spring from. Last I knew Moses Stiltz had brought his hunting dog over for me to train and I watched it sleeping in the corner whilst I was cradling a glass of forgetfulness.

Darla places her hand over mine. *Neither of us are children, now.*

I shunt this to the edge of my mind. Not only isn't this happening, but I'm not wanting this to happen.

Here, she says, *have some lemonade.*

I don't have any money, I tell her, *and besides it's too hot in here.*

She stands, and for one horrible moment I think she's going to remove her pinafore dress. Yet she's only stretching her arms over her head in a yawn.

I've a prank for you, she says. *Close your eyes.*

As I do, I remember all those times I pissed people off and wish those moments could be reclaimed. I hear Stiltz's dog growl in the corner, a guttural sound combined of tension and fear.

When I open my eyes I see there's a bear in the room.

Only it's not a bear. The suit is badly-stitched and Darla's curly locks aren't sufficiently tucked under the mask. Her claws – though – have been manicured at a particularly generous nail-bar.

I watched as she edges towards the dog, which backs up on hind legs only, as though unsure whether to fight or fly.

When she roars, the sound isn't human. I gape as Stiltz's hound hightails it through the open door.

Fuck!

I pass Darla a glass.

This isn't lemonade, she laughs. She flips her face backwards and drinks.

It isn't long before she leaves. I contemplate suicide.

◊

It isn't over yet.

I speak to Roy Rogers, I speak to Jimmy Stewart, I speak

to Henry Fonda. *I need to get the gang back together. I need financing for one last film.*

Poitier and Curtis watch as I walk towards the camera, my posture laconic, a few steps behind the police enforcement officer.

You can see it if you look hard enough, says Poitier. *A kernel inside the nut.*

Curtis nods. *It makes me glad that we were never child actors. Even in comedy I want to be taken seriously.*

Behind me, one truck pulls another. I reach the actors, take off my baseball cap, suggest a whip round.

One last movie, I say. Just the one.

◊

I'm drinking with Spanky. It mightn't be lemonade. After Butch's dog absconded I put adverts in the papers. $50 reward.

Now the dog has been returned and I'm $50 down.

[the audience laughs]

I slap the table top. *It ain't right, buddy.* My speech appears slurred, a problem with the soundtrack. *That dog belonged to Butch. Sure, I lost it but Butch should repay me the reward money.*

Spanky shrugs. *No one will see it that way. And it's Stiltz.*

I'm gonna go over there and get that money even if I have to sing for it.

[more laughter, catcalls of *out of tune*]

I look to the audience. They're older than we are. I realise now that the audience has always been older than us, even when we were the same age.

I swig more lemonade.

Let's head over to Darla's, Butch is there right now.

I see myself rise from the table. My pocket holds the knife with which I once pranked Darla. She told me she might have lost her fingers, when all I lost was her respect.

Darla? Spanky says. *You mean Rita Corrigan.*

There comes a segue which contains the time that we drove, but I have no recollection of this.

I bang on a door.

Let me in [little pig], *let me in or I'll kick your door in.*

My knuckles are black and white.

I'm aware Spanky has a hand on my shoulder. I look at him and wonder at his remarkable resemblance to my drinking buddy, Jack Piott, a still photographer.

Then the door opens and I push pass Darla, and Butch, and I have a little altercation.

I want that fifty bucks you owe me and I want it now.

Butch baulks. *What fifty bucks?*

I swig more lemonade. It's bitter, not sour. I guess we slipped in some rind.

Butch pushes me back. I navigate too many hunting dogs at my feet.

[the audience leans forward]

One of us swings a punch, we grapple. It's *Glove Taps* all over again. I wonder if we're too close to the original, but then Butch breaks and hits me over the head with a glass-domed clock.

[they gasp]

There's blood in my left eye, tainting sepia.

I blink once / twice and Butch emerges from the bedroom holding a .38 revolver.

Unthinking, I make a grab for it.

A shot goes off, fragments the ceiling. The ricochet hits Billie Thomas who I hadn't noticed cowering in the darkness.

Tommy! someone shouts.

[their hearts are in their mouths]

Tommy?

I back Butch into a corner, feel within my pocket for that knife.

I'm going to kill you!

A massive retort.

There's blood coming from my groin.

I see Darla shaking her head.

I see the audience shaking theirs.

[*New York Times: a misfire*]

I wait for the credits.

That's one dark episode.

Then I shake before I drop.

◊

I am livestock fodder.

I'm dead before the hospital. A doctor in a facemask recognises me from those early comedic days. He doesn't believe I look much different.

I force a rictus.

There's that slow, laconic walk. The trucks heading in both directions.

Our Gang.

I was one of those little monkeys.

The defiant one.

1959, June

Oh, Superman

WHEN GEORGE ENTERS the silence cabinet he discovers it horizontal. There is an absence of call-cards, of scuff marks, of cigarette ends sucked to the quick – residues more saliva than paper, of singular sodden rubber rainjackets.

There is an absence.

Perhaps the illusion that lack of gravity buoys, keeps George rotating fast enough to consider making a change. The walls of the silence cabinet are surfaced plush red, the soft-sides of an upmarket loony-bin. The coin box is not in obvious view. The mahogany frame is typical of the straight-grained, reddish-brown timber of the tropical hardwood Honduran species.

George wears a pressed suit, that of a clerk in a newspaper office. He reaches a hand down the serge to his pants leg, takes in a pocket. His fingers enclose. He sorts through metallic shapes, settling on the cost of the journey. A single item.

When he opens his hand he sees the shell casing, hovering a centimetre above the surface of his palm. If he could clutch it he could catch it.

He raises the receiver to his ear.

I want long distance.

Are you receiving me?

◊

Young George runs through the streets of Galesburg, Illinois, over the Underground Railroad. He passes the Gaity Theatre where – in his birth year – the Marx Brothers received their nicknames. He has his own *O*, a hoop with a stick. It bounces over uneven ground and is eventually discarded, describing a parabola as it loops towards the hump yard.

Young George is between fathers right now. His mother bakes cakes and says *hold me*. On hot nights he twists beneath covers, a single sheet sticking to his back. On cool nights, starlight defines features out of shadow, connecting with the stardust of its youth.

Young George runs through the streets of Galesburg. He is a popular child. His friends keep to his pace, as do animals. They cavort at his side within the domain of his dreams. These dreams – these *American* dreams – become *the* American Dream. His mother – who is of German descent – wishes he were *niedergelegt*. Young George wishes he might fly. Yet – years later – he finds he cannot remember if he were at school with Dorothea Tanning.

Young George has his own paintbox. Under the 82.2°F August sunlight he curves an *S* – red on yellow – before completing the black snake tongue. Bare-chested, squatting, bent over paper, heat corrodes his skin. Yet he is indestructible. He leaps building-block cities. He is ignorant of his destiny. A typical force of nature.

Young George writes the initial of his surname – *B* – as though it were an *8*. His teachers desire a straight back, then a double curvature, as though ascending and then descending a fairground slide. George prefers a racecourse. He takes this *B* and treasures it; and when his mother moves them to California maybe she sees something in it because she takes another *B* as her own. George segues from a *Brewer* to a *Bessolo* just as smoothly as the double-*o* of the *8* runs its course. This never-ending pair of circles, this duality of form, similar to two dimes in his pocket, receives him.

◊

So my father, Donald Carl Brewer, married my mother on January 5, 1914. I appeared five months later. What does that tell you about their relationship? My mother never voiced it, but they split shortly after my birth. What does that tell you, again? My father remarried – a second Helen, how unimaginative – and I never saw him after that. When my mother married Frank Bessolo in California I was eleven years old. You know what they say about teenagers, even back then? Yet two years later Frank adopts me. Those were the days.

Good days.

Can we run through that again?

From the start?

From the *teenage* part. We caught some traffic on the tape.

Ok.

(*pause*)

(George looks out the window. Vehicles are increasingly colonising America)

Now?

Now.

You know what they say about teenagers? Yet I hit thirteen and Frank adopts me. Those were good days. Lemonade and sunshine. Football and baseball. Hand in glove. So eleven years follow and I'm visiting relatives and on my return Frank's gone. Gone with the wind. So my mother says he committed suicide . . .

. . . and you didn't know for several years that he was still alive?

I didn't know for several years that he was still alive.

And how did that make you feel?

The suicide? There's all these words, you know: dislocated, angry, disappointed, traumatised, heartbroken, dejected. There's all those fancy words; but if I had to pick one, it would be sad.

Sad. Just sad?

Isn't sad mostly enough?

Okay. So when you hear Frank's still around, that's like a rise from the dead, right? How did that make you feel? Did it make you feel happy?

It made me feel like anything could happen. That maybe death wasn't the end. Is that what you want to hear?

We want to hear it like you tell it.

Then it didn't make me happy. I should have turned to my mother long ago. I should have said, mother, are you deceiving me?

◊

Here in Benedict Canyon I wake to the sound of bees. Through my blurred vision they waggle a figure of eight on the bedspread. Condon once told me that Benedict had managed an apiary so large that he sold 20,000kg of honey from Santa Monica Pier. Now, it appears there are that many bees in my head.

I sort them into groups of four that coalesce and take on human. They're under the floorboards, humming and thrumming. Two are woozy from alcohol and two are mosquitoes in masquerade. The voices confront my anxiety. I'm twenty-minutes slept at twelve-twenty in the morning.

I dumb out the noise remembering my first role: Stuart Tarleton in *Gone With The Wind*. Frank was just around to see it. He was the one told me it was misrepresented as *Brent* Tarleton on the screen credit. Seems like I was destined to play a twosome. To compound the figure of eight I was one half of twins. Fred and I dyed our hair red. We were in the opening scenes. Now I'm in the closing scenes and all I see is red.

I can't shut out the noise.

I'm angry stiff.

Condon is downstairs with Leonore and I know they're sinking beers like they've just stepped off the Titanic, but now Bliss and Carol have joined them and they're gossip heavy. The voices buzz through the wooden boards, as though vibrations from vocoders. Just loud enough to hear, just soft enough to hear nothing.

I get up. Almost pull my underwear over my pants. I'm that tired.

Taking the stairs two at a time I burst into the living room expecting Leonore to say, *Look who it is! Clark Kent or Superman*. But instead I run into Ellanora's arms and we lock each other in a fluctuating false kiss until ten years pass and I finally bob my way back into the present.

But that kiss / perhaps we should have lingered.

◊

George takes a breath outside the *Star Factory*, the Pasadena Playhouse's College of Dramatic Arts. Movie industry scouts were assigned to cover all the productions. Gilmor Brown's singular vision had led to the discovery of many notable actors, playwrights and directors, and eventual entertainment industry giants who went on to establish the Los Angeles empire of film and television, but this isn't why George takes that breath.

He has seen Ellanora Needles – his future wife – for the first time.

She is a blonde with red lips and stylised hair.

He doesn't see much more than that.

O

This is the shape of her mouth when she notices George noticing.

S

This is for *sigh*.

8

Entwine.

Ellanora isn't jealous of Jan Clayton, George's love interest in *Father Is A Prince*, or Rosemary Lane in *Always A Bride*, or Geraldine Fitzgerald in *'Til We Meet Again*, or indeed Lucile Fairbanks, Merle Oberon, Claudette Colbert or Wanda McKay, or indeed any screen actress George encounters during the thirty-one films he makes during their ten-year marriage.

Even so, by the time they separate – childless – it just so happens that George is no longer Ellanora's super man, but is on the brink of being everyone else's.

◊

Narrator: Faster than a speeding bullet. More powerful than a locomotive. Able to leap tall buildings in a single bound.

Man 1: Look! Up in the sky! It's a bird.

Woman: It's a plane

Man 2: It's Superman!

Narrator: Yes, it's Superman, strange visitor from another planet who came to earth with powers and abilities far beyond those of mortal men. Superman, who can change the course of mighty rivers, bend steel in his bare hands. And who, disguised as Clark Kent, mild-mannered reporter for a great metropolitan newspaper, fights a never ending battle for truth, justice and the American way.

◊

"Come here, I've bought you something."

George takes Toni's gloved hand, her fingers all-bone under silk. She is pulling him into her. She pulls him into her for a continued time.

With dry wind buffering their faces, fixing their

expressions, Toni negotiates her vehicle up Benedict Canyon Drive, in the dense hills and narrow, meandering lanes north of Sunset Boulevard.

George has been Reeves for sometime. He doesn't mind the *R*. It's just a *B* with the foundation chipped away. Toni seems to like *R*. She says *R* to George a lot.

George is less understanding of why Toni has taken him under her wing. She is a big player, married to the MGM Studio enforcer Eddie Mannix. Eddie doesn't seem to mind Toni's attention. George is respectful of his young fans. He doesn't smoke in public and Mannix ensures their relationship is media secret. But even so he's only a cardboard figure playing super-possum in the new medium of television. Not that any of it will last.

Toni rounds the corner. Number 1579 is a modest house, with three rooms downstairs and a bedroom and bathroom in the attic.

"How do you like it?"

"I do like it. What is it?"

Mannix laughs. "That's something Clark Kent would say. It's a *house*." She elongates each letter as though spelling it out. "And it's yours."

That pull on his hand. They enter the house. They enter the bedroom. The décor is spotless. There are no bullet holes.

◊

Downstairs is so thick with alcohol that for a moment I forget that they're smoking. Leonore is draped over the small sofa. Condon sits sheepishly on one of the wooden chairs brought in from the kitchen. Bliss and Carol are on the bigger sofa, slumped into each other. They must have been drinking before they entered the house. Condon gives me a look which I can't decide is apologetic or suspicious; as though *he* can't decide if this intrusion is faultless.

When Leonore blinks she releases the tension of our earlier argument. It hasn't been long since Toni occupied that sofa, but the two women are made from different moulds. Whereas Toni is a giver, Leonore is a taker. Knowing this doesn't make me any less stupid.

I nod – once – to the newcomers, then head kitchen-wards to grab a refrigerated beer before returning to the hive.

Carol places her hands in her lap, leans forwards. "Leonore's been telling me you plan to get hitched. Why, congratulations."

I swig from the beer bottle, my tongue briefly stoppering the hole. I can't help but fixate on the penultimate word of her second sentence.

"And then you're taking that stage show to Australia." Bliss voices a statement, not a question. His letters are less defined, corrupted by booze. I take a moment to gather meaning.

"Seems you can't get away from it, lover." Leonore runs her right index finger circular across the top of her bottle. "Superman: the big money spinner."

I don't know why I'm smiling. There's no longer much money in Superman, but we don't have any more. I should be somewhere else at forty-five. If only that low-budget science-fiction film had gotten off the ground. Leonore has no idea of our debt. Maybe that's why I'm smiling. Maybe this transformation has played too long.

I walk as I talk, describe a figure of eight between the chairs and the sofas.

The second beer either numbs or provides clarity.

No one in the room will understand.

Isn't that the beauty of the script?

My only regret will be Toni.

As I head back upstairs, I hear Leonore say, *he's probably going to go shoot himself.*

◊

The bedroom is windowless.

"Did you choose this house so no reporters would ever see inside?"

Toni's head is on George's chest. Transparent love.

She touches his skin with the tips of her fingernails. "Eddie saw to that."

"I've never really understood Eddie."

Toni's gaze follows the path of a bee, tracing a pattern on the white wall. She wonders how it came in here.

"You know the Carnation Milk Company Building? The one that serves as *The Daily Planet*'s front door."

"Of course I do, Clark has been in and out of there a hundred times."

"But only in and out, right? It's an establishing shot." Toni pauses, hesitant. "That's how it is with me and Eddie."

George reaches across to the bedside table, however his lit cigarette has already burnt halfway across and pivoted to stub itself in the ashtray.

"And us, honey, are our scenes interiors?"

Toni is a hard woman. She knows what she wants and she gets what she wants. "I'm here, aren't I?"

But George is aware the relationship is finite. *The Adventures of Superman* is in its sixth series. He's typecast in more ways than one. The duality bothers him. Yet if he can tell anyone what's bothering him, that someone has to be Toni.

"I've changed from Clark Kent into Superman into Clark Kent into Superman so many times it makes me wonder whether each Clark Kent is always the same."

Toni sits. "You been reading Kierkegaard? What about each Superman? You should be reading Nietzsche."

George lights that second cigarette, passes it over. "Superman is one-dimensional. It's that Kent guy I'm interested in."

Toni sucks in smoke. "That man is real. Not made of steel."

◊

THE WEATHER AND
CIRCULATION OF JUNE 1959
A Month With an Unusual Blocking Wave

Extensive blocking during June 1959 culminated in the second lowest 5-day mean zonal index of record for June. Features of the mean 700-mb circulation characteristic of blocking were the out-of-phase, *shattered*, nature of mean troughs and their irregular spacing around the hemisphere. The mean jet maximum was well defined and stronger than normal over the Eastern Pacific and the Eastern

Atlantic. Precipitation was almost non-existent in most of California, whereas rain which fell in Dunstable, Massachusetts was tinted greenish-yellow due to a considerable amount of pollen.

Kent is the first to arrive on the scene. A study in cool detachment. He sees the naked body, shields Lois whose soft footsteps heartbeat the stairs, then slowly closes the door. He makes a note of the 30 calibre (7.65×21mm) Luger pistol at George's feet. Spots the right temple entry wound and the left temple exit wound. Glancing upwards, the bullet in the ceiling. He understands that for George to have his feet on the floor he must have been sitting down when the shot was fired, causing the body to fall backwards on both the bed and the shell casing. Events synonymous with suicide.

Kent spots the unexplained bruises on George's face and chest. The lack of powder on the gun hand and temple. The confusion between the hysterical – inebriated – hive-mind as to Leonore's location when the shot was fired. The possibility of an outside party. He considers the long delay between hearing the shot and calling the police. Events synonymous with murder.

Kent considers Young George would have understood that the only way to return from suicide is not to have committed it in the first place.

Hello?

Hello.

This is long distance. A very long distance.

The *Adventures of Superman* episode titled *The Face and The Voice* features George Reeves in a dual role. That of Kent/Kal-El and Boulder, a thug who undergoes plastic surgery to resemble Superman but who requires a voice coach to sound like him. Kent wonders whether George considered this in his final moments, whether on contemplating the loaded gun he might have repeated:

I look like Superman, why don't I sound like Superman?

Kent concludes his newspaper report. Holds it in memory. He carefully scuffs an *S*-shaped patina of pollen with the toes of his black brogues. From the closet he locates a fresh bedsheet and covers the corpse. Then he turns off the light.

He re-opens the door. Finds a chair in the corner to wait for the sirens. Lois enters and plumps down on his lap. She's silent fresh. He wonders who she resembles in the darkness. Perhaps no one. Perhaps all three of them simultaneously.

She flips out a notepad.

Take this down, she dictates:

The best way to stop a speeding bullet is to catch it dead.

1962

The Girl With The Horizontal Walk

THE HEART WEIGHS 300 grams. The tricuspid valve measures 10 cm, the pulmonary valve 6.5 cm, mitral valve 9.5 cm and aortic valve 7 cm in circumference.

Nicholas Arden looked over the newspaper at his wife, Ellen, buttering his toast at the opposite end of the breakfast table.

"How hard can it be, honey?"

"You haven't read the script. I'll need to dumb down."

"I always said you were too intellectual."

Ellen slid the toast across the table, catching the bottom of the paper. The ink was freshly printed and she imagined some of it colouring the butter. Ellen wondered how much it would take to poison someone. Not that she wanted to poison *Nick*. But she was easily preoccupied.

"I need an angle," she said. "I don't want to be led by the studio on this one."

"Then put your foot down. Both of them, if you have to."

She waggled the butter knife. "Don't get smart, wise guy."

"I'm trying to catch you up."

It was a diamond-bright spring morning. They sat on the terrace extending from their white-painted house under clear blue light. Beneath them, the swimming pool caught ripples off the sky. Somewhere in the house their two children were getting ready for school. Ellen loved them, but she was thankful of the maid. There was only so much morning noise she could take.

Nick folded the paper, wrung out one end with a rueful expression.

"Go on," he said. "You're burning to tell."

Ellen brushed a toast crumb away from the corner of her mouth with her right-hand pinky.

"I play a photographer, Marilyn Monroe. I get to go platinum. Preferably a wig. Marilyn doesn't take great pictures, but she's always in the right place at the right time. Plus she's pretty – we know how many doors that opens, front and back. She carves out a career for herself, *Life, Movieland, Modern Screen*, all those covers. She gets invited to all the right parties, then some of the wrong ones. So there's then a photo of the president, *in flagrante*. Before you know it, she's killed."

"Sounds meaty to me."

"That's just the half of it. There's more. But the dialogue, Nick. It's so corny. I don't know why they've written her this way. It lessens the role."

"How?"

Ellen stood. She ran a hand through her brunette hair, placed another on her hip, pouted: "When you see some people you say, 'Gee!' When you see other people you say, 'Ugh!'"

"I get it. But she's right."

"*She* doesn't exist. That's Schulman."

"The guy with the belly?"

"That's the one."

"And does she talk like that?"

"Like what?"

"In the breathy guttural way you delivered that line."

Ellen sat. "She's such an actress, but she isn't one, you know what I mean? That's how I intend to play her."

"You're an actress playing a photographer as an actress? That doesn't sound like acting to me, honey."

Ellen shrugged. "It's all in the method, Nick. All in the method."

◊

The right lung weighs 465 grams and the left 420 grams. Both lungs are moderately congested with some edema.

She swept onto the lot in her pink Lincoln Capri. A few heads went up. She was running late but they'd factored that in, shooting scenes around her. She twitched her nose, sinuses blocked and hurting. Seeds pollinated the surrounding air. She waved to Cukor then ran to her trailer. Baker was there. She held up a flesh-coloured bodystocking.

"Have you seen this?"

Ellen shook her head. "What is it, a fishing net?"

"It is if you're the fish. It's for the pool scene."

Ellen laughed. "I am *not* wearing that."

Cukor entered the trailer: "My way or the highway, Ellen."

She kissed his cheek. "Is that why you wanted me in the picture?"

He shrugged. "It's a closed set. Only the necessary crew."

"How necessary?"

"It's a pivotal scene. Entrapment. Monroe has the pictures and she wants something from Kennedy. When he arrives she's swimming nude. You don't want to swim *nude*, do you Ellen? I know you crave authenticity."

"I don't remember this scene in the script."

"Schulman's rewriting daily."

"One hand on the table, one under it."

Cukor barked a laugh. "C'mon Ellen. This picture will make you."

"*The Girl With The Horizontal Walk*? I'm already made, thank you. Now I'll be typecast."

Cukor touched her arm. "It is what it is." He put one foot on the trailer step. "They've agreed the wig," he said. "It's in the box. On set in an hour."

Ellen watched the door close. She turned to Baker. "Some day we'll have equal rights."

Baker nodded. She walked over to the box, sucked open the lid. "Here's the wig."

"Here's the role." Ellen took the platinum curls and turned them around in her hands, her fingers becoming entangled in the fabric. "Looks authentic, at least."

Baker nodded, gestured to the chair by the mirror. "Are you ready for your transformation?"

Ellen sat. She closed her eyes, searched for the character. Monroe was there somewhere. It was like peeling an onion. You had to discard the layers until all that was left was raw. Baker elongated her eyelashes, red-lipped her pout, stuck on a beauty spot big enough for a picnic, pinned back her hair and then *pinned* the wig into it. When Ellen emerged from the trailer she *was* the photographer, Monroe, a Konica Autoreflex T Slr 35mm camera dangling off its strap on one finger, white jacket, white blouse, white skirt, white heels. She walked the way they wanted her to, right across the lot. Cukor nodded approvingly, standing to one side as she approached the set. She didn't understand his expression, til he yelled *Cut!* and turning she saw the camera rolling behind her.

"Cukor. I feel violated. I want to be an artist not an aphrodisiac."

"Enough of that. We making a movie or not?"

◊

The liver weighs 1,890 grams. The surface is dark brown and smooth.

Light dappled her body as she turned and twisted under the water. She was embraced. She swam to the bottom, touched it with an outstretched finger, then rose upwards, eyes open. Her breasts were in sway with the motion, the water adding fluidity to their movements, something which rarely happened when wearing underwear. She could see Kennedy standing poolside, his left hand holding his right wrist. Breaking the surface she scattered droplets on his black brogues.

"Hey," she breathed.

"Miss Monroe." He bent and gripped her extended right

wrist, effortlessly hauled her up, residual water stripped from her body as she left the pool, as though she were sloughing a layer.

She stood exposed in the moonlight. She didn't want him to take her, and he had to know that, even though she seemed there for the taking. A couple of inches separated them. She watched him unmoving until goosebumps bumped her dry. Eventually he stood aside and let her pass, handing her a towel which barely covered what he'd seen.

"I thought you might have sent someone."

His jaw was so chiselled he might have auditioned for Mount Rushmore. "I wouldn't miss this for the world."

She walked into the house. Wondered where his body-guards were. "Something to drink?"

Kennedy nodded. Watched her pour a couple of fingers of bourbon. "Nothing for yourself?"

"Maybe when we're done."

"Will we *ever* be done?"

"You'll have it all. The prints, the negatives. I never intended to take those photos. I stumbled into that room."

Kennedy downed the whiskey. "You stumble into black-mail, too?"

Monroe sat down, crossed her legs. "There's a story," she said. "There's a pretty girl on the train, not a beauty, but still something to look at. A guy boards and sits opposite. He's not good-looking either, but he's not bad. After a while he leans over, and says, *I hope you don't mind me saying this, but would you sleep with me for a thousand bucks.* The girl does mind, but she doesn't say anything because the offer has caught her attention. There's something she's wanted to buy, for some time now, a pipedream. And he's polite, not a bruiser. So she says, *yes*." Kennedy watched Monroe's eyes dart around the room. She continued: "So the guy leans back, crosses one leg over the other. *How about for twenty? The girl almost shouts, Twenty! What kind of girl do you think I am? And the man, Mr President, the man says, We've already established what kind of girl you are. Now we're just haggling the price.*"

Kennedy eased himself onto the opposite sofa. He placed his empty glass on a wooden side table with an audible knock.

"What security do you have that I won't kill you?"

She laughed. "I've paid the huntsman."

Outside, dark fell in a torrent, a molasses-thick night. All the lights of Hollywood couldn't penetrate the gloom.

◊

The spleen weighs 190 grams. The surface is dark red and smooth.

"Keep the wig on."

"Oh Nick."

"Just keep it on."

"Hey, you're hurting."

"Ssh."

"Don't *ssh* me!"

"Sorry, losing concentration."

Ellen put her legs over his shoulders. "Fuck her then. Fuck Marilyn."

Nick slid his cock in and out of her cunt. There was something universal in her expression. She was his wife and yet she wasn't his wife.

Ellen did the voice: "I think sexuality is only attractive when it's natural and spontaneous."

"Is that from the script?"

"There's always a script." Ellen put a finger in her mouth and bit. She knew it looked seductive, but it was to keep her from laughing. There was something ridiculous in Nick's ritual determination, something animalistic. She normally loved sex, but getting in Monroe's head had proved anathema. Her character was all about insinuation, but never the act. It was Ellen who had convinced Cukor that simmering heat was better than fire. The script had Kennedy and Monroe making love, but Ellen suggested it should be the mental emasculation of the president which would lead to Monroe's death. Not that it was a death, for she had indeed paid the huntsman.

Nick climaxed and fell on top of her. She tucked her legs around his back, then changed her mind and scissored off him at the onset of cramp. Rolling onto her front she reached out to the side table for a cigarette. "Want one?"

Nick lay on his back beside her. "Let's share. You can take that wig off now."

"Maybe I'll wear it a while. Freak the kids."

"No. Take it off."

Ellen pouted. "What is it now?"

Nick dragged on the cigarette. "There should always be some distance between fantasy and reality. How's the movie going?"

Ellen sighed. "The movie doesn't *go* anywhere, that implies linear motion. We film it in pieces, you know this. Monroe's dead, but then she's already come back, and sometime after she'll also be dead again."

"You never told me what happens after she's killed."

"I was saving some surprises for the premiere."

Nick handed her the cigarette, blew smoke to one side. "Just tell me, Ellen."

She turned onto her back, pulled the sheet over her body. "The president believes Monroe's dead but just like Snow White she's escaped into the forest. She dyes her hair brunette, changes into a plain brown wool suit, spends some time in the Pacific. She could spend all her days there, if she wanted. But she misses the glamour. So she comes back, calls herself Ingrid Tic, gives herself an accent. Fools everyone."

"Except the president?"

"Except the president."

Nick leant on his side. "But what was her story? Where was she *supposed* to have gone?"

"Purgatory or hell. There was a drug overdose. She's supposed to be dead, remember."

"So who *was* dead?"

Ellen furrowed her brow. "The script doesn't make that clear. But when we're filming it's actually Baker."

"Baker? Your make-up girl?"

"She's a ringer, don't you think? They wanted someone who looked like me – like Monroe – but for it not to be me. There has to be a disconnect with the audience, a nudge that maybe Monroe wasn't killed, until it's clear that she's back. So they used Baker. She was right there, after all."

"Baker . . . " Nick mused. "I guess Baker would do it. Did she wear the wig?"

He yelped as Ellen's elbow dug his ribs.

◊

The brain weighs 1,440 grams.

Ingrid Tic knew her way around a camera and a party. She held the viewfinder to her right eye, smiling as she mingled. Everyone wanted to be photographed, their eyes drawn to the lens. So much so that all anyone saw of Ingrid was her upper body and no one paid attention to her walk.

She was a redhead. She had regained the position she had previously held. She'd been reading. *The Last Temptation of Christ*. Chekhov plays. *The Ballad of the Sad Café*. *The Brothers Karamazov*. She had four hundred and thirty books in her library. And for her current role, *The Actor Prepares* by Konstantin Stanislavsky and *To The Actor* by a different Chekhov. On her night table was *Captain Newman, M.D.* by Leo Calvin Rosten. She was making good progress.

Kennedy was there. It had been just over a year. She couldn't resist.

"Mr President!"

Snap.

One of the bodyguards came over, checked her pass. Grunted.

"Oh I know," she said, "you cannot be too careful."

She later realized she had caught his eye.

Everything, including the film in the camera, was loaded.

Ingrid followed her way to the bathroom. A girl on her hands and knees was heaving bile into a toilet bowl. Ingrid urinated quickly in the adjacent stall, rinsed her hands, and checked the mirror. There was no question as to who was staring back. It proved that people only saw what they wanted to see. Was hair colour really that important? Of course, they believed she was dead. Maybe that was the difference. You couldn't expect a person to see someone who was no longer there.

Another girl entered, humming a tune from *Ladies of the Chorus*. That musical must be a decade old. The girl lipsticked her mouth, sang *ev'ry body needs a da-da-daddy*.

Ingrid thought: *sometimes they don't don't don't.*

She watched the girl make-up. The girl glanced at the camera slung around Ingrid's shoulder, then at the girl in the cubicle. Smiled. "Say," she said. "You look familiar. Are you the actress, Ellen Arden?"

Ingrid shook her head. She felt strangely dislocated.

She stumbled out of the bathroom and straight into the arms of Cukor.

Cut! he yelled. *What* were *you doing in there?*

She looked back.

"I was trying," she said. "I was trying to be sick."

◊

The kidneys together weigh 350 grams.

"You've lost more than 25 pounds, I've never seen you so thin."

She poured herself coffee. They could hear mourning doves from the terrace. She glanced down, saw the maid opening the car for the children. "It's the role, Nick. I'm doing it for the role."

"I went down to the lot yesterday. Spoke to Cukor. He says you're not putting the hours in."

She raised her eyebrows, her anger: "Why would *you* talk to Cukor?"

He sighed. "I've seen the rushes. I've seen you. You're not well. You look like a photographer playing an actress as a photographer."

"Being smart doesn't suit you."

Nick shook his head. "Truth is, I'm caught between Ellen and Monroe."

"I'm Ingrid, Nick. *Ingrid.*"

"Are you kidding me? You can't pull this off. Something's got to give."

She looked out from the terrace. In the distance, the Santa Monica mountains. She took another sip of coffee, then turned a semi-circle taking in their apartment's wooden backdrop, the props, the cameras, Cukor, the facsimile.

She held up her hand.

"Can we do this again? One more take? And the script. The script is Goddamn awful."

◊

. . . Monroe wasn't killed. So they used Baker . . .

Cukor spoke to Schulman: "Is this a work of fiction or isn't it?"

Schulman shuffled his notes, a pencil behind his ear. "I'm struggling to remember."

"Just write it like it is. We're never going to finish this picture. We're ten days behind schedule as it is."

Cukor looked out through his office window. Baker was leaning against the side of Arden's trailer, cigarette nonchalant. Arden had yet to arrive. Some mornings she was heavy-lidded. *Who said nights were for sleep?* When she did arrive, Baker spent so long preparing her for the set she might have been embalming a corpse. Cukor stroked his chin. Baker had played a good corpse. But there was more to an understudy than a physical resemblance. Not that Baker *was* an understudy. He wondered if she could be.

"Let me take a look at that script."

Schulman handed it over, watched as Cukor flicked.

It made no sense. Arden was Monroe was Ingrid. Schulman had scored through and rewritten the names so many times that in some places only a hole remained. Baker was written in the margins.

Cukor rubbed his eyes. "What do you think to Baker?"

"Baker? She's plain, stutters sometimes, is overall drab. What are you thinking about Baker?"

"Could we transform her into Monroe?"

Schulman shook his head. "You could never transform her into Monroe. You couldn't even transform her into Ellen."

"*Ellen.* That's what I meant."

Cukor watched as Ellen's pink Lincoln Capri swept onto the lot. She saw him at the window and waved before disappearing into her trailer. Cukor looked at Schulman. "You see that?"

"See what?"

"Ellen just arrived as Monroe."

"So what's she doing now? Transforming back into Baker?"

"Not *Baker*, Schulman. *Ellen.*"

Cukor threw the script to the floor. He left the office and walked across the lot. There was no time for sentimentality. He swung open the door of the trailer. Ellen was surrounded by the cast and crew. Baker held a sheet cake with a naked Ellen drawn on it. *Happy Birthday (Suit)*. Ellen looked Cukor in the eye and smiled. She was undeniably perfect.

In that glance Cukor might have thought *he* was the president.

◊

"8 mg of chloral hydrate, 4.5 mg of Nembutal."

There was a hard pain in her stomach. She looked at her hand holding the Bakelite phone which would soon go out of production. She could barely contain herself.

I'm fired? But I've destroyed the negatives.

"The appendix is absent. The gallbladder has been removed."

Nick!

He looked over the top of his newspaper. The table was set with breakfast things. Fresh coffee. She could smell fresh coffee. Butter was melting into toast.

I paid the huntsman.

"I'm a role," he said. "Haven't you read the script?"

But she had *been reading. Chekhov, Conrad, Joyce. There were four hundred and thirty books in her library.*

"The temporal muscles are intact."

She squeezed her eyes shut. She would count her true friends and everything would be alright. She would count to ten.

One.

"The urinary bladder contains approximately 150 cc. of clear straw-colored fluid."

Two.

"The stomach is almost completely empty."

Three.

"No residue of the pills is noted."

She swung her head around. She'd lost count. Those damn pills. They were supposed to be her salvation.

"No evidence of trauma."

No evidence of trauma! Who said that? Who's there?

Thomas Noguchi, *Deputy Medical Examiner,* looked up from Monroe's body.

"Did you just hear something?"

The man who wasn't Kennedy shook his head.

1967

The Jayne Mansfield
Nuclear Project

Highway 90

W E TAKE IT slow 'round here. We ain't got time for folks can speak languages. We could care less for trained pianists and violinists. Don't give two hoots those studied under Lumet or who can't hold liquor. We're sure ain't darn interested who won Miss Photoflash 1952, no matter how it's shaken up. We make no distinctions. Those journeying from Biloxi to New Orleans just gotta come through. We had no grudges. We take fate as read and plough you into it. If you gotten a mind to, that is.

After The Show

"You got my pink Samsonite, honey?"
    "Right here baby."

"I did good tonight?"

"You did good. They were eating outta your hand. Them lights were low but that guy glowed like an atomic explosion."

"That one I kissed."

"That's right baby. Right on the forehead."

She flipped open the pink Samsonite. The scarlet tag with her name and address embossed in gold shot vertical. She caught it in her right thumb and forefinger. "Heck this is always coming off." She viewed him through the plastic. "You as red as that guy, baby." She pulled her hand back as he tried to snatch it. "Let me get my stuff in here and we can get on the road. Where're the kids?"

"Out back. They're doing fine."

"Tony driving us?"

He shook his head. "Tony's staying behind to arrange the Gulfport tour. Ronnie's doing the driving."

She nodded. "Ronnie's a good guy." She pushed a leopard spot bikini into the back of the case, overlaid it with dresses, sweaters, underwear. "Getting old for this."

He came up behind her. Put his arms either side. Squeezed.

"Says who, baby."

"Says me."

"You need another break."

"I need a picture where I'm more than eye-candy but that bus left a long time ago."

She felt him shrug, almost minimal, as his weight shifted around her.

"You think LaVey will come up with something?"

She laughed. "You kidding." She paused. "He named

me the High Priestess of San Francisco's Church of Satan, but I'm not sure who came best out of that publicity stunt. Me or him."

She pushed down on the Samsonite, secured the silver locks. "Ready to go?"

He moved his hands from her waist, turned them palm upwards. She leant forwards, was cupped. His breath was in her hair. "I don't know whose hardening faster," she breathed. "You or me."

"You or me or me or him."

She wriggled out of his loose grip, turned to face him. With the fingers of her right hand she traced a line down his cheek. "I always wanna stand on tiptoe to kiss you baby."

She did.

He drew back. "We gotta long drive ahead of us."

She raised an eyebrow. Before it could progress the dressing room door banged open and three kids ran in. She smiled, ruffled their hair, kissed the lion-mauled one. "You eaten?"

They nodded.

"Maybe we can stop off later." Like automatic.

She sent them out with Brody. Devoid of life the room became tawdry; like a show with the lights up and the audience seats flipped vertical like multiple lids of pink suitcases. She picked up a lipstick, stood in front of the mirror with its lightbulb arch and coloured herself in. Puckered. *Oh Jayne.* But then Brody was calling and she tripped a switch actuating the explosion of the filament in the third bulb from the right, top line. It wouldn't be noticed til the following day. And even then it wouldn't be *noticed*.

They counted the miles down. Four score and ten.

Tarmac was liquorice black.

Around 2.25 a.m. they sailed over a metal bridge, its steel girders flashing by like sprockets in a film spool. Ronnie depressed the accelerator and they jolted a moment from the surface of the bridge to the regular tarmac of the road. In the back, the kids were sleeping. Ahead, shrouded in insecticide mist, the truck was doing far less than 80. Jayne instinctively reached out a hand, sustaining closed fractures of her right humerus which were insufficient to stop the rest of her propelling where the car had stopped. The top of her head tore away as the vehicle cleaved the underside of the truck. Her wig landed in the footwell.

40-21-35

The heat returned with a vengeance after the thunder-storm, evaporating the road surface with such intent that the tarmac rose with the peeled silhouettes of ghosts. Jayne rolled down the top of the convertible and the wind took her hair. She ran a hand through her brunette locks. She felt good in herself. Tequila burnt a hole in her stomach but her stomach wasn't complaining. Some guy at her shoulder placed a hand on her knee. She didn't know what year it was but it felt like fiction. She'd picked up another beauty competition title, adding Miss Geiger Counter to a list that included Miss Magnesium Lamp and Nylon Sweater Queen. The Cold War might be storming but she was hot hot hot. She stretched her arms upwards, caught the breeze twisting curvatures of air through her fingers. The guy's hand on her knee coursed up her thigh. She let it linger. Felt the sexual energy pulse through his fingers and into the denim material of her jeans.

In a motel she didn't have to hold her breath whilst he contemplated her figure. She held out a hand and led him towards her with her fingers.

Later they dined on 8oz fillet-mignon steaks wrapped in bacon with chef salad, baked potato, sour cream and chives at $2.95 a head. The food was exquisite. She forked some of her potato into his mouth and he cut her a piece of steak. Somewhere, someone was counting something.

On the way to Los Angeles he pulled up at a drugstore and returned with a brown paper bag clutched to his chest. Over a motel room sink she bleached her hair then coloured it platinum blonde, whilst he sank beers on the bed and watched her behind. Later, her hands stretched out to her sides, she giggled as he nuzzled her, one foot against the toilet bowl, wary of contaminating him with those thin rubber gloves.

The weather struck out hotter the further they went. Though her IQ totalled more than her accumulated vital statistics it was clear those in power saw the numbers as high despite the comparison being low.

Cacti populated the desert like hairbrushes. Jayne held an imaginary rifle, took pot-shots.

Going fast, that's the way we go.

"You'll tear into them baby. Like a genetic mutation."

"I like *that* a lot less than Miss Roquefort Cheese."

Acclerate.

"You own the sky."

"Keep talking baby."

She laughed into the wind. A tiny tornado played hide

and seek where tarmac met dirt. She pushed her breasts
forwards with her hands. "I *am* the Jayne Mansfield
Nuclear Project."

"You're explosive."

He wasn't the one who took his eyes off the road, but
she grabbed his hand and placed it between her legs.

Atomic.

Further down they parked up and found a spot in the
desert. The coarse vegetation scratched her buttocks and
thighs and her hair shone like a spotlight. He pushed into
her hard and fast, without remittance, until the sky became
sullen.

Pink Valley

*This here's the Pink Palace, my 40-room Mediterranean-style
mansion.* She swept a hand towards the derelict entrance.
*Pink was my signature colour. I originally chose purple, but
then you know what? I thought purple too close to lavender
and that was Novak's signature colour. You look back now,
you'd never believe pink hadn't been taken, yet I took it and I
must have been successful with it because I got more column
spaces than Kim ever did.*

*This here in the drive is my Cadillac Eldorado Biarritz
convertible; that's the only pink Cadillac in Hollywood. You
dig the tailfins?*

*You'll see I had the whole mansion painted pink, inside and
out.* She continues to walk through the debris. *Those cupids
are surrounded by pink fluorescent lights.* Hargitay himself, my
second husband, built the heart-shaped swimming pool. Aren't
I still married to him? *I wanted galah's for the trees but they*

wouldn't ship them from Australia. Truth or lie? *Here's the interior.* We watch a door fall from rusted hinges. *Take a look upstairs whilst I catch myself some champagne from this fountain.* She shouts as they ascend: *There's pink fur in the bathrooms! And a pink heart-shaped bathtub, matches Hargitay's swimming pool.*

The camera pulls away from close-up. Mansfield is dishevelled. There's a trace of a horizontal scar barely visible through make-up under the hairline of the wig. She leans against the pink fountain gushing alcohol. Footsteps echo throughout the house. She seems startled. As though those footsteps are echoing inside. She sips, then gulps the champagne. Waits for a refill. She's wearing a faded, pink dressing gown, pulled loose at the waist with a frayed cord. Bending forwards she would spill.

Bubbles spark off the fountain like tiny globes rising from molten glass.

Mansfield touches a fingertip to the scar. The camera zooms close. Her face has aged. She traverses the ridge of the scar from left to right. Something like panic seizes her. She looks up the stairs which are no longer there, reduced to meaningless rubble.

I'm confused, she says, and the waver in her voice underlines that confusion just as the scar underlines her death. *Once I was a starlet. Then I was a star. Can you be a starlet again?*

The Church of Satan

"The church does not believe in nor worship the Devil or any Christian notion of Satan."

Jayne watched as LaVey steepled his fingers. She wondered if it were an unconscious movement or whether God exerted an influence for LaVey to turn his fingers inside out and populate the church as in the childrens' nursery rhyme. Yet if this were the case then the spire would be turned upside-down.

"We seek to embrace the Hebrew definition of the word *Satan* as *adversary*. Thus we find Satan represents pride, individualism, and enlightenment: a positive archetype who can stand against organised religion and fight the fears and battle the encouragement to servitude which those faiths seek to impose on us."

Jayne looked around the room. It was theatrically decorated. Two skulls sat on a low table to her right. Sammy Davis Junior had been here.

"Satanism begins with atheism," LaVey continued. "We should acknowledge that we live in an indifferent world. Only then can we shed society's constraints and be true to ourselves."

She nodded: "To feel satisfied with myself is to know that I have arrived."

She wasn't keen on the cape. The horns looked ridiculous. Even if she knew they were just for show.

"If I can cement my belief system within the secularist world-view deriving from natural science, providing an atheistic basis within which to criticise supernaturalist beliefs then I will have done my job."

She was nodding again. "The quality of making everyone stop in their tracks is what I work at."

She stood and LaVey presented her with a medallion and a certificate.

Brody took her arm. "C'mon, baby. We gotta get going."

She smiled at LaVey. "I'm needed elsewhere."

LaVey returned her expression. He was enigmatic, a Mephistophelian rogue. Before she left he bent towards her, whispered in her ear.

It wasn't a word she knew, despite those five languages. But it went something like this: *Erleichda*.

Monroe/Mansfield

They compared her to Monroe but Mansfield had five children and Monroe had none.

Bustin' Out All Over

"Oooooops!"

The paparazzi surged forwards as though a wave whose motions were orchestrated by the twin moons of her breasts.

The polka-dot dress fell to the floor. The music in the Rome nightclub abruptly stopped whilst the soundwaves vibrated without hesitation. Swarthy men stepped forward to help her into it. Flashbulbs split-lit staccato strobes creating jerky puppets in some pre-Švankmajer animation.

"Oooooops!"

The bikini was much too small. Purposely so.

Chlorine stung her eyes as she hit the pool. The red bikini top ribboned away in the water, like a trail of blood from a shark kill.

"Oooooops!"

The dress fell to her waist, twice in almost-quick succession, like scene cuts in a particularly salacious movie.

"Oooooops!"

Loren disdainfully eyed the exposed nipple. *What use talent?* she wondered, aware of the attention that aureole would bring to them both.

"Oooooops!"

Mansfield sat on her pink coverlet with her head in her hands, feet planted on the pink carpet of her pink bedroom. Cotton wool between her toes, nail varnish in hand. Splayed on the carpet lay the Los Angeles Times. Viewed through water she read and re-read: *She confuses publicity and notoriety with stardom and celebrity and the result is very distasteful.*

She whispered: *War is a foolish, childish, animalistic, unthinking, unintelligent way of trying to accomplish a purpose.*

The Jayne Mansfield Nuclear Project

She lay on her back. The sun ripened corn.

In the distance, she could hear her children. Screaming. With laughter.

She shielded her eyes to the glare. An orange glow bled through her closed eyelids. Sometimes she wanted to be invisible but she had read that being invisible included your eyelids and you'd have no protection from the light. Yet, somedays she knew she was the most famous invisible woman and there weren't nothing to shield her from flash-bulbs and publicity and piercing public stares. Sometimes even clothed was to be naked.

She enjoyed her breathing. Thought: How much time aren't we drunk?

Her breasts strained her white cotton sweater, twin

power plants, fuelling her career. She would never know Ballard would declare they loomed across the horizon of popular consciousness, but she did know there was nothing shameful in being a sex symbol.

She sighed and blue sky transformed into dark night and somewhere someone was hauling bodies out of the wreckage and her children her children were all right but Brody and Ronnie were dead and somehow she knew so was she.

LaVey was no more than forgotten.

Her platinum wig – her plutonium wig – lay in the foot-well. The smell of insecticide stung her nostrils. She wasn't all there. Parts of her should have hurt. She wondered if she were exposed.

She closed her eyelids but could see through them. Someone wrote *crushed skull with avulsion of cranium and brain*. A sob wracked her chest, tottered her cleavage. There was a lot of time to be nothing at all.

They gasp.

A smile. There had been much to be thankful for. At the very least she had been nothing short of incendiary. And at the most.

1982

Sarcoline

Wake up.

She sorts through dresses, so many pretty things. Something to remember her by.

She stacks the bed, allows a smile: a slow-mo fade. Their billowed loveliness swells, towers. She considers the fairy tale before clutching them in one scoop and hastening towards the stairwell. Hatboxes line her path, false sentries. She takes steps carefully, her feet hidden. Stephanie is rousing somewhere. There's life to come. She can feel it.

Outside she searches for her metallic green Rover, anticipating it parked out front. The road from the farm winds down the hill and into La Turbie. The day is clement. Behind her the maid has gathered the hatboxes. The driveway is clear. She opens her mouth then hears a discordant scraping sound. The chauffeur emerges from the garage with a chain slung over his shoulder. He leans forwards as he walks, his shoes finding purchase in gravel. Grace watches as the object he hauls comes into view, bound by the chain. She fights understanding. Her chauffeur drags a metal cube pockmarked with upholstery, the furrowed trail in his wake matching her expression. She allows herself to pause.

His expression is grim. It takes him a full four minutes to draw alongside. The maid places the hatboxes on top of the cube, and Grace automatically lays the dresses on top of those. The three of them stand, in regard. Then the maid returns inside the house whilst Grace waits apprehensively for Stephanie. They need to travel from La Turbie, along the D37, for Monaco. They have a train to catch. The average temperature for Paris mid-September is fifteen degrees Celsius. They can't miss it.

◊

Wake up.

Her favourite actress is Ingrid Bergman and her favourite actor Joseph Cotton. She considers her parents broadminded though her father believes acting is a slim cut above a streetwalker, despite Grace being named after his sister, an aspiring actress who had died at the age of twenty-three.

In her room at the Barbizon Hotel for Women she lays diagonally across the bed. The tape recorder squeaks on rewind. She simultaneously presses record and play. Speaks: *fairytales tell imaginary stories. Me, I'm a living person. I exist.* On the bed beside her lies the script for Strindberg's *The Father*. She reaches for a pencil and taps it against her teeth. Her legs extend upwards, crossed at the ankle. Within a coffee cup, dregs congeal. This scene is lit by the non-Technicolor glow of her bedside lamp, its shade muted yellow as the beam.

Night glazes her window in a neon-illumined oil slick. Downstairs, she can hear men leaving. The hotel maintains a strict curfew. Some of the residents consider this an inconvenience, but Grace appreciates the benefit. There are plenty of other places if required. She lives on the third floor of the salmon-coloured building and a further twenty floors extend above her. Sometimes she equates the size of the building with the potential for her career. She is done with fresh-faced modelling in beer and insect spray advertisements; even if they had their uses. She can't be photographed by clever men without learning her good and bad points. So she sweeps her hair back from her face, wears the minimum of make-up and avoids sarcoline-coloured high heels that would falsely accentuate height. Grace defers to effortless elegance. She wants nothing tawdry in her life.

Rolling onto her back she extends a yawn, covers her mouth. The ceiling is high. She closes her eyes, imagines herself weightless, ascends. Traffic noise punctuates the silence. Her recorded voice in the role of Bertha approaches from the bed. Grace repeats words within her head: a human echo. In the street a crowd gathers, pointing towards her bedroom. Her closed eyes allow no perception. Gradually, once dialogue is stored to memory, she discovers that the bedsheets have risen, warming beneath her. She opens her eyes, heads towards the bathroom.

The door opens inwards but doesn't budge. Grace leans against it with her right shoulder, shoves. There is no understanding. Her immaculate forehead creases. Perhaps something has fallen, lodged on the other side.

She considers which of her beauty products might wedge. The telephone on her bedside table forms a question mark, but she decides against calling for the janitor because she is wearing a pale pink nightdress made of the finest silk.

Eventually her shoulder begins to bruise, fresh blood leaking into her tissues. Day and night interplay as the reddish iron undergoes a transformation to purple, then metallic green, and finally a dull yellow-brown. She keeps her body to the door, fluctuating between attempted ingress and preventing exit. Her imagination spirals between cause and substance. Pressure builds in her skull; an abhorrent certainty. Fear coalesces, forms a cube.

Grace sinks to her knees, places an ear against the wood. Listens.

◊

Wake up.

Mogambo *had three things that interested me: John Ford, Clark Gable, and a trip to Africa with expenses paid. If the movie had been shot in Arizona I wouldn't have done it.*

My character had a rival in Honey Bear. Rivals weren't anathema to me but it's not true to say that I thrived on them. Of course older men are more attractive, who would say otherwise? If they happen to be married then that's their business, not mine. Don Richardson, Gene Lyons, Gary Cooper, Clark Gable, Ray Milland, William Holden, Bing Crosby, Oleg Cassini . . . stop me before I run out of fingers. Psychiatrists would say those relationships were a way of seeking the approval and love my father withheld from me, but they won't admit a natural predilection. Hitchcock was fascinated by this inherent contrast of sexual elegance, and said so. Me? I was simply me.

The studios are tenacious. When they want someone or something, they usually get it in the end. I signed the contract with MGM at the desk of the airport, when the engines of the African plane were already turning.

Thika was my favourite location, with the Fourteen Falls a magnificent backdrop. I'd sit and watch those native tribes perform their music that incorporated the soundtrack, wondering whether they would ever receive adequate royalties. Ford might have been a bully, but in this industry the bullies are those who know what they want – whatever the cost. I've been described as intelligent and professional, but thankfully never a bully. That's because I've realised Hollywood doesn't have all that I want.

In Mogambo *my husband was played by Donald Sinden, who Ford treated disgracefully. Donald had to have his chest hair removed because Gable – who wasn't hirsute – considered it a slight if other actors had a masculine advantage. But the funniest part was that Francoist Spanish censors wouldn't allow adultery to be shown onscreen and so Donald and I were dubbed as brother and sister in the Spanish version. That's what I've come to call a sarcoline moment, where appearance can be augmented by artificiality without the mechanics being noticed. Like in a cheat.*

What's that you have there? An African Brown-headed parrot? I'm afraid I don't recall those when shooting Mogambo. *There were so many birds. The comparison with my sarcoline moment? That the colour descriptive is only twenty per cent of the bird when the majority of its feathers are a bright metallic green? Well, yes, it is beautiful, but do you mind removing it? No, I can't tell you why, but it's just that . . .*

Yes, I came to success too quickly. Perhaps too quickly to value its importance.

◊

Wake up.

"Honey, is that a gun in my pocket or am I just pleased to see you?"

"Oh Ray, don't be silly."

"I'm paraphrasing you, dear."

"Paraphrasing me? What am I supposed to have said?"

Milland walked across to the cabinet and mixed them both drinks. She considered him accomplished in his dinner jacket and tails. They were close to finishing *Dial M For Murder*. She loved the title. She loved Ray.

"You said: Mr Hitchcock taught me everything about cinema. It was thanks to him that I understood murder scenes were to be shot like love scenes and love scenes like murder scenes."

He returned with the drinks, sat down on the arm of her sofa. Though it wasn't her sofa, as such, but that which resided in her hotel room. The area was spacious, yet her interest lay in the space between them.

"Is this a murder scene?"

"If you like."

Milland bent and kissed her, his lips approaching slow motion. Cue tremor.

She reciprocated, drew heat into her body. Her fingers clutched, pressed. Time was an escalation. "Oh Ray."

"Yes."

"I'm expecting him to make his cameo."

Milland laughed. He walked across to the window. They were fifteen storeys high. An expanse of sky threatened to suffocate the city. Black cars ran like beetles on the street. It had only been seventy years since both height and motorisation had combined in such a resonant cliché. Ray considered everything that had passed and everything that he supposed was to come. They were but a pinprick of existence. Under those considerations, his adultery was so insignificant as to hold no significance. He had yet to inform Grace that his wife, Mal, had thrown him out of the house. No doubt he would do so, eventually.

Grace stood behind him. She reached around and clasped his chest, fingers finding buttons.

"What is this?"

"I'm searching for a concealed weapon."

They laughed. Turned to kiss. "I never thought you'd stoop to B-movie."

"Oh Ray. We need a better scriptwriter. The plot isn't so bad, just the dialogue."

Milland pivoted his left thigh between her legs. She felt the urgency, but didn't have the prescience.

They fucked with abandon. She pulled the bed sheets from four corners for the maid to ball and wash.

Later, alone, the tabloids revealed their unkindness. She tore out a page suggesting she was a home wrecker and screwed it into a clenched fist. Gossip columnist Hedda Hopper spread rumours she was a nymphomaniac. Milland ended the relationship when he realised how much it would cost him in a divorce. The edges of the torn paper hurt her palm. When she opened her fist she saw the literary fragment was more of a cube than a sphere. Tears weren't slow to tumble. Grace watched them discolour.

◊

Wake up.
   "Ten minutes Miss Kelly."
   "Thank you boy."
   Her timing was out of her hands. She had been in make-up since seven-thirty and would remain there until done. A girl fussed her hair. Punctuality was keen, she was no Monroe-diva, but even minimal couldn't be rushed. The true transformation, however, was internal. Hitchcock had declared, *She'll be different in every movie she makes. Not because of make-up or clothes, but because she plays a character from the inside out.* Grace was fond of the man.
   Yet there was less fondness for the movies. She perceived a shelf life. In her previous film she was in make-up from eight. Joan Crawford had been in from five, and Loretta Young since four in the morning. *I'll be god-damned if I'm going to stay in a business where I have to get up earlier and earlier and it takes longer and longer for me to get in front of a camera,* Grace had said, uncomprehendingly selfishly. *I'm ready to leave.*
   She couldn't deny the costumes were tremendous. She loved her golden gown for the film's costume ball, and had a long friendship with her designer, Edith Head, even if Edith were a nemesis with regards to weight.
   "You're perhaps a little too short-waisted and long-legged."
   "I'm doing my best with my waist, but can't do much with my legs."

"That's not quite what I've been hearing."

Their laughter was companionable. Grace wondered about her reputation. Films and costumes would last, wouldn't they? Forays into the darker pages of the tabloids were temporary imaginings. Success wouldn't be measured in newsprint but the perfection of celluloid. She said as much to Edith.

"My dear, you will be remembered longer than my creations. And in the best possible way."

Five minutes Miss Kelly.

Her hairdresser gave the nod. Grace rose from her seat, journeyed the lot. Scenic backdrops were propped by wooden posts. She walked through the artifice, considered it mirrored. Normally there was bustle, but people appeared absent. She became caught in patterns of disorientation, repetition siding against her. Eventually, as though perforating bubble-skin, reality burst. She glimpsed the back of the director's chair with the familiar name scribed in black on white. Hers alongside.

There was some difficulty due to her gown, but she gently lowered herself onto the green canvas. With the quick snap of a seasoned professional, the chair folded with her inside it, enclosing her within a square, deconstructing her bones.

She could only watch as she was gripped, carried, and dropped into the Mediterranean Sea.

◊

Wake up.

"If the story of my life as a real woman were to be told

one day, people would at last discover the real being that I am."

Edward Quinn nodded. He had been given the job of photographing the meeting of Grace Kelly and Prince Rainier of Monaco for *Paris Match,* as part of a piece on the Cannes Film Festival. After an inauspicious start where his Peugeot ran into the back of the MGM hire car carrying the actress towards the palace, they had arrived to find the Prince absent. Quinn suggested they might take some pictures inside, and by the time the Prince arrived Grace had visited practically every room.

It was a horrid, horrid morning. After I showered I discovered there was a power cut at the hotel, meaning I couldn't dry my hair nor press my clothes. I improvised a pulled-back coiffure and donned my only unwrinkled outfit. It was a silk taffeta dress with a print of large cabbage roses and a flowered headband, much less subtle than my usual pared-down preference.

Grace had been happy to take the tour. Quinn noticed with pleasure how photogenic and beautiful she appeared. She understood the mechanics of modelling and there were no histrionics or excessive demands which he sometimes experienced with other actresses. In one shot he positioned her between two large mirrors, her right hand resting lightly on a polished tabletop. She stared elegantly, perhaps wistfully, into the distance as her image was repeated six-fold; each succeeding image slightly out of focus, suggesting the presence of future selves.

The photographer had me regarding figurines and statues, as though I were an antiques expert sent to value goods and chattels after a death. I attempted nonchalant intelligence, but I feel the pictures appear quixotic in hindsight, and if my life hadn't changed irreparably after that day they would be catalogued as faintly ridiculous. You might say – although I wouldn't – that I entered into the marriage purely to retain the prophetic beauty of those images. Am I allowed to think that?

Quinn found a certain formality in the sword room that countered the floral pattern on Grace's dress. There were over fifty displayed exhibits. Quinn was particularly taken by an arrangement of ten swords in an unintentionally exaggerated *fleur de lis*. He knew that sometimes connections between subject and object are forged by the photographer, by the act of photography.

I remember a model boat, probably the length of me, in a glass case. The photographer spent an age capturing my reflection but he would never have known what I was thinking.

When Prince Rainier arrived, one hour late, when they were on the verge of leaving, Quinn prided himself on taking the exact photograph of their first meeting: Grace, her knee bent in a very discreet American bow, shaking hands.

He maintained a personal zoo. He petted a baby tiger. I thought, now there is very a charming man.

When Grace Kelly married Prince Rainer of Monaco in April 1956 her shoe designer, David Evins, hid a copper penny inside her right shoe for good luck.

Perhaps there is discolouration. I understand copper can tarnish through oxidation, which removes electrons from the surface. That would explain its greenish hue. But what makes no sense is the apparent change in shape.

◊

Wake up.

Memories accessed through cootie catchers. She thinks, she blinks, they change.

I have two children. It is 1962.

Hitchcock wants me for Marnie *but Monaco won't have it. They don't know what they're missing.*

Margot Fonteyn is teaching us The Twist. *Rainier hates public dancing, so we're in our private apartment with dear Joan and Martin. None of us can get the hang of it. There is so much laughter. Margot says, "It's easy, just pretend that you're stomping out a cigarette with one foot, and drying your back with a towel at the same time."*

Suddenly: effortless.

I have one child. It is 1957.

Caroline is ten months old. Rainier is delighted. He wants an heir.

I am pregnant. Rainier runs a hand along my belly, a miniature ski-slope.

Rainier: my only desire is loving you eternally.

I have three children. It is 1970.

We're having a ball. Gregory Peck sits to my right. I wear a white dress complemented by ruby earrings and a white floral fascinator. Gregory's attired in a simple dinner jacket and bow tie. How lucky I am to be a woman, unlimited by formality even on formal occasions.

I have no children. It is 1956.

My Prince has allowed MGM to film our wedding in exchange for ending my seven-year movie contract.

Our detractors have said that my life will end upon marriage, but that's only because they want me for them. They can still love me. But I will only love him.

I have two children. It is 1962.

Rainier sits solo in their private apartment, a glass of brandy cupped in his palm with all the delicacy of a cradled fontanelle. Their acquaintances, the Americans Joan and Martin Dale, are on the adjacent sofa, their legs angled towards each other. Grace has stood to retrieve her book of horoscopes. She likes matching guests to star signs, is intrigued by comparisons.

Her own sign is Scorpio. She read at a young age that she would be defined by outward shyness and inner determination and took pleasure in accepting that fact. Finding her page she reads, You are inclined to like lampshades with plastic covers. *She laughs, as do her guests.* "How did they know?"

I have three children. It is 1982.

I sort through dresses, so many pretty things. I pile the back seats. The absence of space forces me into the driver's seat. We hit the road and the road hits back. So much to think about my brain haemorrhages. Just pretend that you're stomping out a cigarette with one foot. *We can't miss it. We surge through the low retaining wall, are catapulted one-hundred-and-twenty-feet through tree branches down the slope. Sight becomes a sea of green.*

The idea of my life as a fairy tale is in itself a fairy tale.

◊

Wake up.

Oh please. Wake me up. Wake me

Concordance

Albuquerque – the most populous city in the state of New Mexico. Bugs Bunny should have made a left turn there in 1945.

Angeli, Pier – Italian-born actress romantically linked to James Dean. Died of accidental barbiturate overdose aged 39.

Angelus, The – an oil painting by Jean-François Millet, completed between 1857 and 1859.

Arden, Ellen – fictional character played by Marilyn Monroe from the unfinished 1962 movie *Something's Got To Give*. The film was abandoned after Monroe's death, although she had already been fired from the production.

Arden, Nicholas – fictional character played by Dean Martin from the unfinished 1962 movie *Something's Gotta Give*. The film was abandoned after Marilyn Monroe's death, although she had already been fired from the production.

Baer, Max – an American boxer who once dated Jean Harlow. Died of a heart attack aged 50. His last words – reportedly – were *Oh God, here I go*.

Baker, Gladys Pearl – mother of Norma Jean Baker. Died of old age, aged 81.

Baker, Norma Jean – actress most commonly known as Marilyn Monroe.

Ballard, J.G. – English novelist. Died of prostate cancer aged 78.

Balloonatic – nickname attributed to Roscoe 'Fatty' Arbuckle.

Barbizon Hotel for Women – from 1927 until 1981 this building operated as a residential hotel for women, with no men allowed above the ground floor.

Bast, William – American screenwriter and author who roomed with James Dean at UCLA. Died of Alzheimer's disease aged 84.

Beginner's Luck – a 1935 *Our Gang* short comedy film directed by Gus Meins. It was the 135th *Our Gang* short and marked the first appearance of seven-year-old Carl 'Alfalfa' Switzer and his ten-year-old brother Harold Switzer.

Bern, Paul – American film director, screenwriter and producer, married to Jean Harlow. Two months after their marriage he was found dead of a gunshot wound under suspicious circumstances. There was no suggestion Harlow was linked to his death. He was aged 42.

Bliss, William – one of several people present at the house party during which George Reeves shot himself. Fate unknown.

Blood and sand – cocktail made from ¾ oz blended scotch, ¾ oz blood orange juice, ¾ oz sweet vermouth and ¾ oz Cherry Heering.

Bond, Tommy – an American child actor known for playing Butch in the *Our Gang* series of comedies. Died of complications due to heart disease aged 79.

Boxing Match – a combat sport usually between two men who throw punches within a square known as a ring. Rudolph Valentino won a boxing match against the *New York Evening Journal* boxing writer, Frank O'Neill, over a slight by an anonymous writer for the *Tribune*.

Brody, Samuel – Jayne Mansfield's lawyer and alleged lover. Died in the car crash which killed Mansfield.

Buttocks – Fatty Arbuckle once suffered second degree burns to both buttocks due to an accident on set.

Cannert, Jules – a Romanian artist known for his *pulp* covers for magazines such as *Breezy Stories*, *Droll Stories* and *Dreamworld*, as well as a reputation for romantic pastel portraits of glamorous Hollywood stars. Died aged 64.

Carmen, Jewel – Silent film actress and wife of Roland West. Died of lymphoma aged 86.

Carnation Milk Building Company – Building used as establishing shots for the *Daily Planet* newspaper in the long-running *Superman* television show.

Caveat lector – let the reader beware

Coca-Cola Bottle – a design intended so that *a person could recognize (it) even if they felt it in the dark, and so shaped that, even if broken, a person could tell at a glance what it was.*

Cocoanut Grove – nightclub within the Ambassador Hotel, Los Angeles, frequented by many movie stars from 1921 until it was demolished in 2005. In 1968 Senator Robert F. Kennedy was assassinated there in the hotel's main kitchen.

Coin – unit of money often tossed to determine a choice from two options. *Heads* or *tails* representing the result of a 50/50 gamble. Additionally, an old Irish tradition holds that placing a coin in the heel of a shoe will bring a bride much luck and happiness.

Columbo, Russ – American singer and actor who was fatally killed aged 26 in a peculiar shooting accident when a gun being cleaned by a friend went off. He had been romantically linked to Carole Lombard. His death was concealed from his mother for the last ten years of her life.

Condon, Robert – American writer who was present at the house party during which George Reeves shot himself. Fate unknown.

Corrigan, Rita – wife of Moses Stiltz, the killer of Carl Switzer. Fate unknown.

Cukor, George – American film director. Died of a heart attack aged 83.

Curtis, Tony – an American film actor. Amongst his many movie roles was that of John "Joker" Jackson in *The Defiant Ones*. Died of a cardiac arrest aged 85.

Dale, Joan – friend of the actress Grace Kelly and wife of American diplomat Martin Dale. Author of *My Days with Princess Grace of Monaco: Our 25-Year Friendship, Beyond Grace Kelly*. Died in 2005.

D'Amore, Pasquale "Patsy" – legendary restaurateur who introduced the New York-style pizza to Los Angeles.

Day Dreams – title of Rudolph Valentino's book of poetry.

Day For Night – the cinematographic technique of shooting night scenes during the day.

De Saulles, Blanca – a Chilean heiress and friend of Rudolph Valentino, who fatally shot her ex-husband following a custody battle. Died of barbiturate overdose aged 45.

Dees, Mary – an American actress primarily known as a stand-in for Jean Harlow in the film *Saratoga* following Harlow's death. Dees herself died after a long illness aged 93.

Delmont, Bambina Maude – friend of Virginia Rappe, against whom California police had filed at least fifty counts of extortion, bigamy, fraud and racketeering.

DiCicco, "Pasquale" Pat – an American agent and movie producer, also an alleged mobster working for 'Lucky' Luciano. Died aged 67.

Dildo – a sex toy, usually phallic in shape. Actor, Roman Novarro, is said to have kept a black lead Art Deco version embellished with Rudolph Valentino's silver signature.

Double Whoopee – a 1929 Hal Roach Studios silent short comedy starring Laurel and Hardy, with a cameo from Jean Harlow.

Douglas DC-3-382 – airplane carrying the actress Carole Lombard and other passengers which crashed into the Potosi mountain range, killing all on board.

Erleichda – last words attributed to Albert Einstein in the Tom Robbins' novel, *Jitterbug Perfume*. Loosely translated as *Lighten Up!*

Eureka Café – fictional café featured in the *Roy Rogers Show*.

Fairmount High School – high school where James Dean was first exposed to acting, now demolished.

Fichte, Johann Gottlieb – Eighteenth century German philosopher. Amongst other writings he argued that "active citizenship, civic freedom and even property rights should be withheld from women, whose calling was to subject themselves utterly to the authority of their fathers and husbands." Died aged 51.

Fishback, Fred – American film director, actor, screenwriter, and producer. Friend of Fatty Arbuckle. Died of cancer aged 30.

Flappers – a generation of young Western women in the 1920s who wore short skirts, bobbed their hair, listened to jazz, and flaunted their disdain for what was then considered acceptable behavior.

Fonteyn, Margot – English ballerina who taught Grace Kelly how to twist. Died of cancer aged 71.

Ford, John – American film director who first noticed Grace Kelly. He said that she showed "breeding, quality and class". Died of stomach cancer aged 79.

Gable, Clark – American film actor often referred to as "The King of Hollywood". Gable was romantically linked to many Hollywood actresses and was married five times – his third wife, Carole Lombard, died in a plane crash on her way to his arms. Gable died of a heart attack aged 59.

Galah – also known as the rose-breasted cockatoo, the galah can be found in almost all parts of mainland Australia.

Glenn, Barbara – one time girlfriend of James Dean. Fate unknown.

Grauman, Sidney – American showman. Died of a heart attack aged 70.

Great San Francisco Earthquake, The – San Francisco, California, was shaken by a massive earthquake on the morning of April 18th, 1906. Whilst it lasted less than a minute it ignited several city fires and destroyed almost five hundred blocks.

Guinness, Alec – English actor with a much respected career, who had a premonition of James Dean's death by car crash. Died from liver cancer aged 86.

Harrison, Ronnie – driver of the 1966 Buick Electra 225 which was involved in the car accident which killed Jayne Mansfield. Harrison was also killed in the car crash.

Hawks, Howard – American film director, producer and screenwriter. Died from complications arising from a fall when he tripped over his dog, aged 81.

Head, Edith – American costume designer, who won a record eight Academy Awards for Best Costume Design. Died of bone marrow disease four days before her 84th birthday.

Heart of a Gypsy – song sung by Thelma Todd from *The Bohemian Girl*, left in the movie after her appearance was cut from the film following her death.

Hell's Angels – Howard Hughes directed movie starring Jean Harlow but not Thelma Todd.

Hickman, Bill – professional stunt driver who worked on films such as *Bullitt* and *The French Connection*. He was the first person on the scene at James Dean's death. Died of cancer aged 65.

Highway 90 – one of the major east-west U.S. Highways in the Southern United States, runs through southern Louisiana for 297.6 miles, serving Lake Charles, Lafayette, New Iberia, Morgan City, and New Orleans.

Hitchcock, Alfred – English film director and producer. Died of kidney failure aged 80.

Hood, Darla – an American child actress best known as the leading lady in the *Our Gang* series. Died from acute hepatitis from a blood transfusion during an appendectomy aged 47.

Hopper, Hedda – American actress and gossip columnist. Died of double pneumonia aged 80.

Hudson, Rock – American actor – born Roy Scherer Jr. – who felt it necessary to hide his homosexuality within the Hollywood film industry. Died of AIDS-related complications aged 59.

Hunter, Tab – American actor, pop singer and author – born Andrew Klem – who acknowledged his homosexuality in 2005, confirming rumours that had circulated at the height of his fame. Died after suffering cardiac arrest that arose from complications related to deep vein thrombosis, aged 86.

Jayne Mansfield Nuclear Project, The – line from the song, *Confessions of a Psycho Cat* written and recorded by The Cramps.

Joyita – merchant vessel owned by Roland West from which 25 passengers and crew mysteriously disappeared in 1955. The boat was found adrift in the South Pacific with no one aboard.

Kennedy, John F – American president who served office between January 1961 until November 1963. Conspiracy theorists link him to the death of Marilyn Monroe. Died of assassination from a gunshot wound at the age of 46.

Kerry, Norman – actor and friend of Rudolph Valentino. Died from a liver ailment aged 61.

Laurel, Stan – an English comic actor and film director who would rather have skied than died. Died of a heart attack aged 74.

Lavender Marriage – a male-female marriage in which one or both of the partners is homosexual or bisexual.

LaVey, Anton – founder of the Church of Satan. Died of pulmonary edema aged 67.

Lemmon, Leonore – society playgirl who was in a relationship with George Reeves at the time of his death. Died of complications related to alcohol dementia aged 66. Her body was discovered five days after her death.

Lemonade – any sweetened beverage characterised by lemon flavour. A lemonade stand featured prominently in the *Our Gang* episode, "The Lucky Corner".

Lincoln Phaeton – an automobile built by the Lincoln Motor Company. The actress Thelma Todd died in such a vehicle from carbon monoxide asphyxiation.

Lion-Mauled – Jayne Mansfield's son, Zoltan, was attacked by a lion named Sammy while he and his mother were visiting the Jungleland USA theme park in Thousand Oaks, California. He suffered from severe head trauma, underwent a six-hour brain surgery, and contracted meningitis. He thankfully recovered.

Lubitsch, Ernst – a German-American film director, producer, writer and actor. His films were described as having "the Lubitsch touch". Died of coronary thrombosis aged 55.

Luciano, Charles "Lucky" – An Italian-American mobster considered to be the father of modern organized crime in the United States. Died of a heart attack aged 64.

Lupino, Ida – an Anglo-American actress and singer. Died of a stroke aged 77.

Mannix, Eddie – American film studio executive and producer, remembered for his work protecting Hollywood stars as a "fixer": a person paid to disguise details of the stars' often colorful private lives to maintain their public image. He allegedly approved of the affair that his wife, Toni Mannix, had with George Reeves.

Mannix, Toni – American actress and dancer notorious for an extramarital relationship with actor George Reeves. Died of Alzheimer's disease aged 77.

Marx, Groucho – Born Julius Henry Marx, Groucho – with his trademark cigar and moustache – was the wise-cracking quick witted member of the Marx Brothers. Died of pneumonia aged 86.

Mathis, June – an American screenwriter, who wrote films such as *Blood and Sand* (1922). Died of a heart attack aged 40.

McFarland, George "Spanky" – American actor famous for his appearances as a child star in the *Our Gang* series of comedies. The term "a spanky child" was slang for an intelligent, gifted toddler. Died of a cardiac arrest aged 64.

McPhail, Addie – the third and final wife of Fatty Arbuckle. Died of natural causes aged 97.

Methylenedioxymethamphetamine (MDMA) – a drug commonly known as ecstasy.

Milland, Ray – Welsh actor and film director. Although never admitted by either, rumours were rife that Grace Kelly and Milland were engaged in an affair during the filming of *Dial M For Murder*, fuelled by notorious gossip columnist Hedda Hopper. Died of lung cancer aged 79.

Mineral City – fictional city featured in the *Roy Rogers Show*.

Navarro, Ramon – Mexican actor portrayed by MGM as the *Latin Lover*. Inspiration for Charles Bukowski's short story, *The Murder of Ramon Vasquez*. Died of asphyxiation due to murder, aged 69.

Needles, Ellanora – wife of George Reeves. In her later years she served as a religious minister. Died aged 83.

Negri, Pola – a Polish stage and film actress romantically involved with Rudolph Valentino. Died of pneumonia aged 90.

New Amsterdam Theatre – building on 214 West 42nd Street said to be haunted by the ghost of Olive Thomas.

Niedergelegt – German word meaning *laid down*, carries the intimation of *calmed*.

Oh, my God – the words Olive Thomas is purported to have said as she realized she had inadvertently drunk poison.

One Dollar – to leave someone one dollar in a will was believed to effectively disinherit them.

Our Gang – a series of American comedy short films about a group of poor neighborhood children and their adventures, created by comedy producer Hal Roach.

Pickford, Jack – actor, brother of Mary Pickford, lover of Olive Thomas. Died of progressive multiple neuritis aged 36.

Pink Palace – in 1957 Jayne Mansfield bought a 40-room Mediterranean-style mansion at 10100 Sunset Boulevard in Beverly Hills, California. Mansfield had the house painted pink, with cupids surrounded by pink fluorescent lights, pink fur in the bathrooms, a pink heart-shaped bathtub, and a fountain spurting pink champagne. She called the abode her "Pink Palace".

Piott, Jack – Unit still photographer who was with Carl Switzer the night he was shot. Fate unknown.

Platinum Blonde – a song by the pop group, Blondie, recorded in 1976.

Poitier, Sidney – a Bahamian-American actor, film director, author and diplomat. Amongst his many movie roles was that of Noah Cullen in *The Defiant Ones*. Died of cardiopulmonary failure, aged 94.

Porsche 550 Spyder – a racing sports car produced by Porsche between 1953-1956. Perhaps the most famous of the first 90 Porsche 550's built was James Dean's "Little Bastard", numbered 130 (VIN 550-0055), which Dean fatally crashed into Donald Turnupseed's 1950 Ford Custom at the CA Rte. 46/41 Cholame Junction.

Potosi – a mountain about 30 miles southwest of Las Vegas and the site of an air crash which killed 22 passengers in 1942, including the actress Carole Lombard.

Powell, William – an American actor who was married to Carole Lombard. Following their divorce he was subsequently involved with Jean Harlow who died before they could marry. His distress over her death led him to accept fewer acting roles. Died of heart failure aged 91.

Pre-Code – refers to films made prior to the enforcement of the Motion Picture Production Code censorship guidelines. Movies made between 1920 and mid-1934 often included depictions of sexual innuendo, miscegenation, profanity, illegal drug use, promiscuity, prostitution, infidelity, abortion, intense violence, and homosexuality.

Prince of Whales – nickname attributed to Roscoe 'Fatty' Arbuckle.

Quinn, Edward – photographer who captured the first meeting of Grace Kelly and Prince Rainier of Monaco. Died aged 77.

Rainier III, Prince of Monaco – ruler of the principality of Monaco for almost fifty-six years and internationally known for his marriage to American actress Grace Kelly. Kelly ceased making movies upon their marriage. Died of a heart attack aged 81.

Rambova, Natacha – American film costume and set designer married to Rudolph Valentino. Died of a heart attack aged 69.

Rappe, Virginia – American model and silent film actress. Died of a ruptured bladder and secondary peritonitis aged 26.

Red Rose – a perennial flowering plant placed annually by a woman in black at the crypt of Rudolph Valentino.

Roach, Hal – an American film and television producer, director, and actor, best known today for producing the *Laurel and Hardy* and *Our Gang* film comedy series. Died of pneumonia aged 100.

Rogers, Roy – cowboy actor and singer who went on hunting trips with Carl Switzer and assisted him in getting parts in his television show. Died of congestive heart failure aged 86.

Rover P6 3500 – car which Grace Kelly was driving when she had her accident in Monaco. The vehicle was metallic green in colour and subsequently crushed, cubed, and dropped into the Mediterranean sea.

Rowboat – Usually a small wooden boat propelled by oars, such as that used by Jean Harlow's mother – also Jean Harlow – in a rescue bid to remove her daughter from Camp Cha-Ton-Ka in Michigamme, Michigan, after she became ill with scarlet fever.

Samsonite – An American luggage manufacturer and retailer.

Schulman, Arnold – American playwright, screenwriter, producer, songwriter and novelist who co-wrote the unfinished movie *Something's Got To Give*. At the time of writing, Arnold Schulman remains alive.

Screwball – cocktail made from grenadine, lime, orange juice and vodka.

Selznick, David O – American film producer. Died of a heart attack aged 63.

Sewing circle – a phrase coined by the actress Alla Nazimova to represent a discreet code for lesbian or bisexual actresses.

Sheridan, Liz – one time girlfriend of James Dean, most familiarly known for her role as Helen in *Seinfeld*. At the time of writing Liz Sheridan remains alive.

Sherman, Lowell – American film actor and director and friend of Fatty Arbuckle. Died of pneumonia aged 49.

Shovel-Snouted Lizard – Latin name *Meroles anchietae*, this African creature prevents its feet from burning on hot sand by adopting a thermal dance.

Silence Cabinet – alternative name for a telephone kiosk designed so that background noise does not interfere with a call.

Star Factory – Name for the Pasadena Playhouse's College of Dramatic Arts, attended by George Reeves amongst many others. The Playhouse remains in existence.

Stephanie, Princess of Monaco – the youngest child of Rainier III, Prince of Monaco, and American actress princess Grace of Monaco. At age 17, Stephanie was involved in the car crash that unfortunately killed her mother. At the time of writing, Princess Stephanie remains alive.

Stiltz, Moses – owner of a hunting dog trained by Carl Switzer. Stiltz shot and killed Switzer during an altercation over money. An inquest considered this self-defence. Died aged 62.

Strindberg, August – a Swedish playwright. Died of pneumonia complicated by stomach cancer aged 63.

Superman – comic book character created by writer Jerry Siegel and artist Joe Shuster. Superman was born Kal-El on the planet Krypton before being sent to Earth as an infant. Superman is most vulnerable to green Kryptonite, mineral debris from Krypton transformed into radioactive material by the forces that destroyed the planet.

Syphilis – a sexually transmitted infection which actor Jack Pickford denied he was suffering from.

Thelma Todd's Sidewalk Café – a successful establishment in the Los Angeles coastal neighborhood of Pacific Palisades. There were 270 stairs from the garage to the entrance.

Thomas, Billie – an American child actor best remembered for portraying the character of Buckwheat in the *Our Gang* series of comedies. Died of a heart attack aged 49.

Tic, Ingrid – fictional character played by Marilyn Monroe from the unfinished 1962 movie *Something's Got To Give*. The film was abandoned after Monroe's death, although she had already been fired from the production.

Today Is Tonight – a novel written by the Hollywood actress, Jean Harlow, which remained unpublished until 1965. Its average rating is 3.2/5 on Goodreads.

Traje de luces (suit of lights) – traditional clothing worn by Spanish bullfighters in the bull ring.

Trigger – palomino horse belonging to singer and actor Roy Rogers. Trigger could sit in a chair, sign his name "X" with a pencil, lie down for a nap and cover himself with a blanket. Died a day short of his 31st birthday. After his death, Rogers opted to have him mounted in his iconic rearing position.

Twist, The – a dance inspired by rock 'n' roll music which became the first worldwide dance craze. It goes like this.

Un Chien Andalou – short surrealist film made by Luis Buñuel and Salvador Dali in 1929, the opening scene features an eye cut open by a razor.

Underground Railroad – a network of secret routes and safe houses established in the United States, used by African-American slaves to escape into more accommodating areas.

Underwear – Thelma Todd, Marilyn Monroe and Jean Harlow were all allegedly advocates of the wearing of no undergarments.

Valentino's syndrome – pain presenting in the right lower quadrant of the abdomen caused by a duodenal ulcer with perforation through the retroperitoneum.

Van Ronkel, Carol – one of several people present at the house party during which George Reeves shot himself. Fate unknown.

Vargas, Alberto – a noted painter of pin-up girls, including the painting of silent film actress Olive Thomas, titled *Memories of Olive*. Died of a heart attack aged 86.

West, Roland – Hollywood director known for his proto-film noir movies. Ended his career following the Thelma Todd scandal. Died of cardiovascular disease aged 67.

What can happen on a plane? – line cut from the movie *To Be Or Not To Be*, following actress Carole Lombard's death in a plane crash.

Wills, Beverley – one time girlfriend of James Dean. Fate unknown.

Winkler, Otto – actor Clark Gable's friend and publicist who had a fear of flying. Died in a plane crash aged 39.

Wütherich, Rolf – German automotive engineer and racer who was a passenger in the car James Dean crashed, sustaining a double fractured jaw and serious hip and femur injuries. Died in another car crash aged 53.

Ziegfield, Florenz Jr – the Broadway impresario noted for his revue show, *Ziegfield Follies*. He was known as *the glorifier of the American Girl*. Died from pleurisy aged 65.

Contributors

Fatty Arbuckle was born Roscoe Conkling Arbuckle in 1887 in Smith Center, Kansas. He was one of the highest paid movie stars of his generation until scandal wrecked his career. Whilst he was completely exonerated after three trials, his career never completely recovered. Arbuckle died of a heart attack in 1933 just as a new contract suggested his star might regain ascendance.

James Dean was born James Byron Dean in 1931 in Marion, Indiana. He made three feature films in quick succession between 1955-1956, before his death in a car crash cemented his legendary status.

Peg Entwistle was born Millicent Lilian Entwistle in Wales, UK, in 1908. After finding Hollywood success elusive she committed suicide in 1932 by leaping from the letter *H* on the iconic Hollywoodland sign.

Jean Harlow was born Harlean Harlow Carpenter in Kansas City, Missouri, in 1911. She enjoyed a successful movie career until her death in 1937 at the age of twenty-six of cerebral edema. One of the MGM writers said, "The day Baby died there wasn't one sound in the commissary for three hours".

Grace Kelly was born Grace Patricia Kelly in Philadelphia, Pennsylvania in 1929. She made eleven movies – three directed by Alfred Hitchcock – winning an Academy award for best actress for *The Country Girl* (1954). She retired from acting upon marriage at the age of twenty-six. In September 1982 she suffered a stroke whilst driving leading to a near fatal car accident. Following a second stroke whilst in hospital the decision was made to turn off her life support machine. Consumed with grief, her husband, Prince Rainier of Monaco, arranged for her car to be crushed into a cube, taken out into a deep section of the Mediterranean, and sunk.

Carole Lombard was born Jane Alice Peters in Fort Wayne, Indiana, in 1908. She was the highest paid star in Hollywood in the 1930s. In January 1942 she tossed a coin to decide whether to take the train or a plane to return home to husband Clark Gable from a charity event in Indiana. The plane crashed into the Potosi mountains, killing everyone on board.

Jayne Mansfield was born Vera Jayne Palmer in Bryn Mawr, Pennsylvannia in 1933. She was a major Hollywood sex symbol of the 1950s and early 1960s and enjoyed commercial success on Broadway as well as in the movies. Renowned for her *wardrobe malfunctions* and excessive publicity, Mansfield died in a car crash in 1967 when the vehicle she was travelling in smashed into the rear of a slower-moving vehicle.

Marilyn Monroe was born Norma Jeanne Mortenson in Los Angeles, California in 1926. Starting out her career as a pin-up girl she soon moved into movies and her first breakthrough role came in *The Asphalt Jungle* (1950). She catapulted to stardom through a succession of major movies although became disillusioned at being typecast as another dumb blonde. Married three times, Marilyn was found dead in her apartment in 1962, apparently as a result of accidental barbiturate overdose. Conspiracy theories abound which challenge this view.

George Reeves was born George Keefer Brewer in Woodstock, Iowa, in 1914. Typecast as Superman in the long-running television series he died via a gunshot wound in 1959. The official finding was suicide.

Carl Switzer was born Carl Dean Switzer in Paris, Illinois, in 1927. At the age of six he secured a role as Alfalfa in Hal Roach's comedy series, *Our Gang*. His tenure ran for six years until the show folded, but adult roles proved to be less forthcoming. In 1959 he was fatally shot by an acquaintance over a dispute concerning money.

Olive Thomas was born Oliva R Duffy in Charleroi, Pennsylvania in 1894. She enjoyed a successful silent movie career from 1916 onwards until her untimely death in 1920 of acute nephritis after consuming mercury bichloride. The death was ruled accidental, but was the subject of much media speculation and has been cited as one of the first heavily publicised Hollywood scandals.

Thelma Todd was born Thelma Alice Todd in Lawrence, Massachusetts in 1906. She successfully transitioned from the silent film era to the talkies, mostly through slapstick comedy roles. Also a successful businesswoman, Todd died as a result of carbon monoxide poisoning in 1935 only nine days before Christmas.

Rudolph Valentino was born Rudolfo Alfonso Raffaello Pierre Filibert Guglielmi di Valentina d'Antonguella in Castellaneta, Italy in 1895. A sex symbol of the 1920s, this 'Latin lover' starred in several silent films before his death from peritonitis in 1920. An estimated 100,000 people lined the streets of Manhattan to pay their respects at his funeral.

Acknowledgements

ALL STORIES ARE copyright 2022 and previously unpublished except for the following:

'Memories of Olive' copyright 2018. First published in *Ambit #231*.

'The Girl With The Horizontal Walk' copyright 2019. Previously published as a chapbook by Salò Press and reprinted in *Best British Short Stories 2020* (Salt Publishing).

'Sarcoline' copyright 2016. Previously published at Great Jones Street and reprinted 2018 in the anthology *Norwich* (Dostoyevsky Wannabe Press).

I would like to thank the following for their enthusiasm for these stories - either individually, or as a collection - since I began this project:

Kelly Abbott, Nina Allan, Briony Bax, Georgina Bruce, Ray Cluley, Homer Flynn, Andrew Humphrey, Kate

Acknowledgements

Pemberton, Marcus Reichert, Nicholas Royle, Priya Sharma and Tim Shearer.

And to Christopher Hamilton-Emery and everyone at Salt who loved this collection and ran with it.

Additional thanks to Sophie Essex aka Felix aka Little Fish for her constant support, both personal and editorial. This one is most definitely for you.

This book has been typeset by
SALT PUBLISHING LIMITED
using Granjon, a font designed by George W. Jones
for the British branch of the Linotype company in the
United Kingdom. It is manufactured using Holmen
Book Cream 70gsm, a Forest Stewardship Council™
certified paper from the Hallsta Paper Mill in Sweden.
It was printed and bound by Clays Limited in Bungay,
Suffolk, Great Britain.

CROMER
GREAT BRITAIN
MMXXII